SERPENT
darling

PANDORA
CRESS

First edition: October 2024

Cover Design: Plot Twisted Designs

Formatting: EJL Editing

AUTHOR'S NOTE

This book is a mix of Contemporary and Dark Romance.
I like to call it Dark Romance (Lite) because those un-familiar with Dark Romance are not likely to find anything very triggering. I aimed to create a fun and fast-paced book that would introduce darker themes to new readers while keeping it appropriate outside of those genres. With that being said, there are still themes and elements that one may have strong feelings about and so I will list those that I think are important to note.

Intense Sexual Situations
Toxic Parents
BDSM
Consensual Sexual Violence
Mentions of Drug Use
Gang Depictions
Excessive Swearing
Smoking
Off-Page Murder
Other Woman/Other Man Drama

Songs I Want To Fuck To

Genghis Khan

Miike Snow   3:45

< ◀◀ (▷) ▶▶ ♥

SCAN HERE

Backstage
NEFFEX ♥

La La Lh
The Dirty Youth ♥

Where Did The Party Go?
Francois Mercer ♥

Lying Is The Most Fun A Girl Can Have Without Taking Off Her Clothes
Panic! At The Disco ♥

Granite
Sleep Token ♥

Fire Escape
Andrew McMahon ♥

I Touch Myself
Dyvinyls ♥

Dress
Taylor Swift ♥

Hotter Than Hell
Dua Lipa ♥

It's Hard To Say I Love You When You're Sitting On My Face
Marty & The Mufftones ♥

I'm A Sucker For A Liar In A Red Dress
Adam Jensen ♥

A Bar Song (Tipsy)
Shaboozey ♥

BAR & CLUB

*To the filthy souls seeking solace in these pages from your
dimly lit corners of the world,
This book is my toast to you.
May the smoke-filled air of The Serpent Pit cloak you in
desire and the clink of whiskey glasses be a siren's call to
your wild, untamed hearts.
So, grab a seat. This drink's on me.
Cheers, motherfuckers.*

ONE

The Serpent Pit was bustling with chatter and music as Jagger Wilder deftly poured drinks and slid them down the polished wood of the bar to a rowdy group of men. They laughed and jostled each other, sloshing their beers as they snatched up the frosty mugs. Jagger grinned, his eyes glinting under the neon lights advertising various liquors and brews.

This was his domain now.

What was once the trashy biker bar where illegal activity ran rampant, had quickly grown to be one of the most popular watering holes in Jersey.

As the men toasted and downed their drinks, Jagger scanned the room, finally coming to rest on Sadie Sweetwater perched atop a barstool near the end of the bar. A stack of papers sat in front of her and she chewed on the end of a pen, brow furrowed in concentration. Jagger smiled softly, taking in her honey blonde hair that she kept tossing back over her shoulder when she leaned forward to write. She was stunning even in her focused state. "Hey boss, another round over here!" one of the men called out, breaking Jagger from his thoughts. He cleared his throat and moved down the bar to top off their drinks. As he worked, he kept glancing back at Sadie. His mind wandered to memories of their complicated past.

They'd met in their Sophomore year of college during an English Literature class that was a test of their mutual patience. The professor had been lacking in the department of anything that pertained to their class on the best of days, and they found themselves griping over assignments they'd already been through in High School.

It started off with them meeting for coffee on Tuesdays and Thursdays before class to stimulate their own brains, do creative writing exercises, or discuss the reading assignments since their professor barely went over anything. Instead, Mrs. Tinney seemed content to water her plastic plants, put on a movie adaptation of a book, and call it a day most of the time.

Jagger mentioned that one day, he saw a flask on her desk when he shuffled in early to ask about an upcoming paper. She hid it in her desk as he made his way over to her, though, and ignored the situation entirely.

"How is she still allowed to work here?" Sadie muttered one day as they walked down the pathway to the next building, where their other classes resided. She looked over at Jagger, who had amusement dancing in his eyes, and they both blurted out, "Tenure," before dissolving in a fit of laughter.

It was a fast friendship, and they got along better than most. They challenged each other where school was concerned and in their everyday lives. They held each other accountable and moved through the semesters at NYU with grace and determination. They dated a few people while at college, but nothing serious. They chalked up the good and bad experiences to life lessons and kept their private lives relatively separate from whatever they had.

When Jagger's dad decided to run off to Arizona at the end of his senior year to pursue his new female obsession with his younger brother, he'd asked his son to run his bar for the time-being. It wasn't the worst idea, and Jagger was thankful he could take the apartment upstairs and say farewell to living on campus. The only problem was that he'd have to move back to New Jersey and that he would be short-staffed with his dad and brother gone. Only a few people felt comfortable working at the Serpent Pit and dealing with the fights and gangs it brought in, so most of the staff included locals or members of the Renegade Rebels, which Jagger was a part of, or the children of them.

When Jagger told Sadie about his situation, she immediately offered her help.

It was an easy decision. Sadie's mother lived in New Jersey and ran the local paper there. She'd told Jagger about it being a good opportunity for her to hone her editing skills working for her family before stepping out into the big bad world in a year or two. It was another thing they learned they had in common - growing up in the same town. It never bothered them that she was born on the right side of the tracks and he was from the wrong side. Sadie blew into the Serpent Pit and cleaned the place up, literally and figuratively. Having a pretty blonde from the suburbs of North Ward in Newark brought in a mixed crowd and more business. She mostly bartended with Jagger during the evenings after helping out her mom at The Upside Scoop, but on occasion, she would audition dancers for the weekend shifts, helping them learn some basic pole dance moves and how to handle themselves around the men who may have had a few too many.

"Jagger, you got a minute?" Sadie's voice cut through the noise and in turn, his memories. She waved him over, tapping her pen on the papers.

"What's up?" He leaned on the bar across from her, trying not to get distracted by a loose strand of blonde hair that curled against her cheek.

Sadie pointed out a few items on the schedule, clarifying when certain deliveries were expected and asking if he could get Gremlin to cover a shift later that week. Jagger nodded along, the familiar cadence of her voice washing over him. But he found himself zoning out, enraptured by the way her green eyes sparkled when she laughed, and the curve of her lips as she spoke.

"Jagger? Did you hear me?" Sadie asked, arching an eyebrow.

"Huh? Oh yeah, sure thing," Jagger mumbled, shaking himself out of his daze.

Sadie gave him a confused smile and went back to her paperwork, mumbling that they needed to hire more dancers soon.

"What was that?" He asked, the music of Fall Out Boy too loud to hear what she said.

"We need to post auditions again. I only have a few girls on the schedule this week and we should have a dozen in rotation."

Jagger sighed and glanced at the papers in front of her. "We could just... not have dancers. Put in another pool table or something."

Jagger had wanted to do without the dancers and take the pole down since he got the keys to the place. He wanted to avoid the headache of needing to keep bouncers in the club at all times, but Sadie kept having to remind him it would be a wrong business move.

"The girls keep the men calm, Jag," she explained, gesturing with her hand towards a group of men who were playing pool together and hooting at one of the regular dancers.

The young brunette girl was distracting a burly man from the fact that he'd just scratched on the 8-ball. His curses were caught in his throat as she shimmied in his direction, flashing him a pretty smile and a wink.

Jagger pinched the bridge of his nose and closed his eyes for a second. He knew she was right. "Fine, but you have to handle the auditions on your own this time. I'll pay you extra for it, it's just that I don't feel comfortable sizing these girls up. Makes me feel like a creep," he shrugged as Sadie laughed.

"You don't have to pay me extra, Jag. I'm happy to help. Just let me use the pole sometimes after work. I don't get much time to run to the gym, so I'd like to do some dancing when we close."

"Just some extra time here?"

Sadie nodded as she sorted through the papers on the bar top, organizing them in a neat little pile.

Jagger tried not to think of Sadie, scantily clad, playing around on the pole after the bar was cleared out. "Why do I think you've already been doing that, Sadie?" He smirked at her, and she looked up from her reading to give him a mischievous grin.

"What the boss doesn't know, won't kill him," she said and felt intense satisfaction at the groan he made when she held the papers up between them as a makeshift barrier. She loved to tease him and had years of practice to know how to get under his skin. When she flashed him a flirty wink over them he snatched the paperwork from her hands and started making his way towards the office in the back.

"Not true, Sweets!" Jagger yelled over his shoulder as he unlocked the door to the office.

"That mental image is definitely going to kill me," he whispered to himself as he rushed in, closing the door behind him quickly before she could tell by the shape of his pants how much his body was responding to his thoughts. Fuck. You'd think he'd be over this little infatuation after all these years, but here he was. A fucking embarrassment, adjusting himself like he had just heard about porn for the first time.

Jagger tossed the schedule onto his desk and rubbed a hand over his face tiredly before sitting in his oversized leather desk chair and propping his feet on the ledge. The material was warm when he reached into his black leather jacket pocket and pulled out a pack of Camel Menthols. He lit one and inhaled deeply as he leaned back and looked up at the ceiling. Jagger wasn't sure when he developed feelings for his female counterpart, although part of him felt like they'd always been there. He simply assumed that part of him knew better than to act on them and ruin anything and just kept hoping that part would continue to make the right call.

Sadie was also in a steady relationship right now, the first one since he'd met her.

When they returned home to New Jersey, her mom had set her up on a blind date with a nice guy named Travis Colm. He coached the Central High Fox's football team and was great at it. He was an excellent cook. Full of charm and charisma, Travis had a tall, athletic build that filled out his tanned frame and accentuated his short blonde hair and hazel eyes. He always helped out at school events. It seemed Travis was more than capable at everything.

Except for pleasing Sadie, Jagger would come to find out.

Chapter TWO

"Can you grab their orders, Sadie? I gotta get a couple more cases of beer to put in here." Jagger spoke loudly over the music in the bar from his crouched position, sizing up the empty spaces through the clear glass doors of the cooler.

He cocked his head towards the door to the men who had just walked in when Sadie turned to look over her shoulder from where she was at the small sink behind the bar washing glasses.

"Sure, Jag," she said with a smile. She dried her hands on the dishcloth that was sitting on the counter in front of her before making her way toward the customers, wiping her hands as she greeted them. Her blonde hair fell in soft waves around her shoulders, framing her face and Jagger loved the fact she literally let her hair down when she was around him.

That tight ponytail was reserved for the outside world but not here in his. Although there were more than a few times, he imagined fisting that same ponytail in his hand as he fisted his own cock for release.

Jagger allowed himself a second to stare at her round ass as she walked around him before getting to his feet and making his way towards the stockroom, where they kept their extra coolers and freezers full of beer and liquor. Sadie only wore black at work, sporting her Serpent Pit crop top, jeans, and motorcycle boots. Jagger had frequently teased her that she had no right buying them unless she would let him take her for a ride on his bike, but she rolled her eyes and stuck her nose in the air, commenting on how it was for the aesthetic and good tips. He would never admit it to her, but those fucking boots did things to him.

Sadie poured three pints of Guinness and set them down on the coasters she had laid out on the bar top.

"Anything else I can get you, fellas?" She asked with her signature bright smile.

One man started to say something that would have undoubtedly led him into trouble, but his friend elbowed him in the ribs with a sneer, "We're good, doll. Thanks."

As Sadie walked back to the sink to finish cleaning the glasses, she nearly bumped into Jagger, who stood with two large cases of Yuengling, and vaguely heard the gentlemen whispering behind her.

She couldn't make out much, but she did catch, "Don't fuck with the bartender. I like it here, and the Wilder boy will kick you out for life."

At that moment, Sadie met Jagger's eyes, and he gestured to the cases with a nod of his head. She helped him set them down and went to work stocking them with him before asking, "Is that true?"

Jagger didn't look up from his task and simply asked, "Is what true?"

Sadie let out an exasperated sigh. "Have you been exiling the customers that have been fresh with me?"

Jagger shrugged and closed the cooler door before helping Sadie to her feet. When he tried to move past her, she stepped before him and gave him an expectant look.

"Yes," he finally answered, looking into her bright blue eyes again.

"Jesus, Jag! You can't do that," Sadie snapped at him. "There's always going to be jerks in a bar."

Grabbing his hand, Sadie turned him back around to face her when he went to walk away from her.

"What would you do if they touched me?" She implored, digging deeper. "Would you punch them or something?"

Jagger thought back to one particular time last year when she first started working with him, and a drunk grabbed her ass when she had brought some drinks to his table. She had managed to sidestep the next advance that was coming between her legs and turned on her heel before she had calmly gone over to Gremlin, who worked as a bouncer on the weekends. When she explained what happened, he made his way over to tell the gentleman and his friends that their drinks were on the house, but they had to leave.

Jagger watched from behind the bar and met Gremlin with the man in tow at the doorway.

"I'll take it from here," Jagger said, escorting the guy and his friends out to the parking lot.

You could still hear the music blaring from inside the bar as he held the backseat passenger door open for the asshole and helped him inside. His friends piled inside the car, and when the engine kicked on with a loud roar, Jagger leaned down to whisper in the asshole's ear. "It's a shame no one ever taught you to keep your hands to yourself, but I like giving lessons."

The guy looked up at him, his hand on the back of the seat behind him and the other on the door frame. Jagger slammed the door shut suddenly, crushing the man's hand against the frame before ripping it open and tossing his mangled hand onto his lap while he let out a pained scream.

"Get home safe, now," Jagger smiled to the men, who looked at their friend in shock and then back at him.

They peeled out of the parking lot after that.

"Yeah, probably," he agreed, returning to the present.

Sadie's laughter was unexpected, but she probably thought he was kidding.

Let her think what she wants, Jagger thought, and leaned against a cooler.

One of the shot girls bounced over to the opening in the bar and turned her attention to the handsome bar owner.

"Can I get some more shots, Mr. Wilder?" She grinned and gestured to her tray of empty shot glasses she had sold on the floor that evening.

"I can do that for you, Bianca," Sadie offered kindly, reaching with her hands for her tray.

Bianca shoved her hand into her bra which looked to be purple under the blacklights and pulled out a bunch of dollars before pushing them into Sadie's outstretched hands.

"You can put that in the register," Bianca quipped before looking at Jagger with a slow smile and lowering her voice. "I would rather have Mr. Wilder fill me up."

Sadie blinked twice and opened her mouth to say something before she stomped towards the register. She glanced at them while un-wrinkling the crumpled dollars and putting them in their respective slots in the register. Bianca was still openly flirting with him, placing her hand on his arm while he poured whiskey into a new set of shot glasses on a tray. Jagger laughed at something she said and stole a glance at Sadie, who glared back in return, slammed the cash register shut, and took off towards her sink to finish her glasses.

Sadie was really starting to hate the new shot girl.

Chapter THREE

"Hey, baby," Travis waved at Sadie when he entered the bar, pushing past a few college kids from town waiting on their Uber to take them back to campus.

Sadie gave them a soft smile and reminded them to take some tylenol when they got in safe as they passed by Travis on their way out. Her eyes trailed over to Gremlin who was standing by the door making sure no one else came in as they cleaned up for the night. Gremlin was close with Jagger but he didn't say much, just worked security on busy nights and helped out when needed. He was intimidating like a giant, black, fearsome force to be reckoned with. But those who knew him personally would tell you that he had 3 little sisters at home he took care of after his mother passed, his favorite drink at the bar was a Sex on the Beach, and that he got his name because his favorite Christmas movie was Gremlins. He threw a smile at her once the door closed behind the last of the customers, but Sadie didn't miss the glare he gave Travis as he made his way towards her.

She was still behind the bar, wiping off the bottles in preparation for the next day. "How was your night?"

He settled into a stool before her and rested his forearms on the bar. Sadie smiled at Travis before she looked over at Jagger, who was helping Bianca with her coat at the back of the establishment. It was April, but the cold weather hadn't gone away yet.

The gorgeous red-head was toying with her zipper, and Sadie suddenly wished she could hear what they were talking about but turned her attention back to her boyfriend.

"It's been long," she sighed, putting the bottles back on their respective shelves. "I'm excited to go home."

Travis pouted, "I thought we were going to go back to my place tonight?"

"We can still go to your place, if you want. I'm just really tired. I figured I should go back to mine since I'm probably going to crash the second I see a bed."

Sadie looked at the clock on the wall near the bar's entrance, which was flashing bright and pink at 2:23 A.M.

"You can come to my place and sleep, babe. I won't bother you tonight," he joked and winked at her.

Sadie gave him a forced smile and started gathering her stuff from behind the bar. She pulled a hair tie off her wrist and quickly threw her golden tresses into a ponytail before putting on her coat and placing her hand in Travis's as they made their way to the door.

"I'll see you tomorrow, Jag!" She called out in his direction as they walked out of the Pit, forcing herself not to look at him and Bianca as she blatantly flirted with him in the dimly lit bar.

That night she ended up back at Travis's place, and despite her wishes for a good night's sleep, it had led to sex.

Sadie didn't love Travis, but she did like him. He was kind to her, did all the right things, and her family adored him. They had been together for a little over a year, and it was going well to everyone outside of their relationship. It might have worked if he had any interest in her hobbies or favorite things—or better in bed.

No, Sadie's mind corrected. *He's not bad in bed; you just don't know how to orgasm from sex.*

Travis got Sadie off with his fingers a few times and his mouth about a dozen. But with his dick? Not once.

He was too soft in bed, all light strokes and kisses. He would whisper words of adoration, and his touches were always gentle. Whenever she tried to encourage him to go faster, he went slower.

Sadie wanted to throttle him.

So tonight, she had finally decided she'd been silent on the matter for too long. Especially after the jealousy little Miss Bianca had brought out earlier. What kind of fucking name was Bianca, anyway? She needed some sort of a release and was getting desperate.

Propping herself up on her elbows, she leaned over his chest as he tried to catch his breath and asked, "Can we talk?"

Travis smiled at her and responded, "Of course, babe. How was it?" He slid his hands up to her waist and pulled her closer to him.

Sadie put on her best smile, totally aware she was faking everything at this point and not just her orgasms. "Great."

She rested her chin in her hand, her right elbow digging into the mattress, and ran her left hand down his chest. "I was just thinking, what would you say to try some stuff out? Like maybe something a little rougher." She paused when she saw the look on his face. "I mean, maybe some new positions or, like, maybe you could try spanking me?"

"Oh my god, Sadie. Why would you want me to hurt you?" Travis asked in shock, his hands flying to her shoulders. "Are you feeling alright?"

Sadie bit the inside of one cheek to keep from screaming at him and took a deep breath.

"I'm not asking you to punch me in the face, Trav. I'm trying to see what else we might be good at together. We should be open to trying other things," she tried to explain carefully, aware of his hands gripping her shoulders and searching her face with his eyes.

"I don't know, Sadie." Travis sighed. "I think we have amazing chemistry in bed. We change positions a lot. It's not always me on top; sometimes we switch, and you get to be on top."

Sadie grimaced but covered it with a cough.

Silence was the best option at this point.

He didn't get it, and he wouldn't get it.

Travis pulled her back a little to look into her eyes, and when she met them with her gaze, he asked quietly, "Is this about Jagger?"

Sadie sat up so quickly she almost fell out of his bed. "What? Why would you even say that?"

She pulled his blue comforter up to her naked chest as his hands fell back against the sheets. Travis pushed himself up on his forearms and gave her a sideways glance.

"Are you serious? He's the ultimate bad boy," he laughed as Sadie scrunched her nose up in confusion. "He's in a gang, runs a bar, is smart, rides a motorcycle, smokes, and can drink most men under the table. He's literally a modern-day James Dean."

When Sadie tried to laugh it off and roll her eyes, Travis pushed onward. "And I saw how you were looking at him and that new girl when we left."

Sadie averted her eyes briefly as she thought about what he said. Back in college, she had considered him a potential lover, but their friendship was too important to act on it. Plus, he never really gave her a reason to think he was all that interested in her. Her brain, of course. But her body?

"That's ridiculous. Jag's my friend; I could never think about him like that. I just don't like that girl and think he can do better."

Sadie moved onto her side and tucked her arm under her pillow, bringing it into a higher position.

"It's just... I heard some girls talking at the bar tonight about some stuff and thought it was interesting."

Sadie kissed his cheek, and he smiled before remarking and patting her head, "We're fine just the way we are."

Travis hugged her close, and Sadie waited until his deep breathing assured her he was asleep before throwing her clothes back on and sneaking out into the living room. She couldn't rest right now with her thoughts a mile a minute. Sadie would have killed for a beer, but this was Travis' apartment. So, there was wine.

Copious amounts of wine.

But nothing else.

Nothing stronger, nothing more satisfying.

Sadie let out a huff and swiped some stray hair out of her face that had escaped her ponytail. It all just seemed to be one giant metaphor for her perfect, wholesome relationship.

Eventually, she grabbed water from the fridge, went over to his gray couch and sprawled out on her stomach. Her work clothes from that evening still smelled of smoke and whiskey. Her favorite scents.

After a few minutes of mindlessly scrolling through Facebook, she saw an ad for an app called "SecretScape" - *A place to escape your secrets*. What a tagline, she thought, but curiosity got the better of her when she hit the download button.

Settling on the simple screen name of **Bookworm-Barbie**, taking delight in the comparison of her persona, name, and interests. Once the profile stats were out of the way (opting not to disclose anything except that she was a female in her twenties), she got to the main screen and saw dozens of boxes with text.

They all contained dirty secrets.

Some were pretty tame, like 'I lost my virginity to my brother's best friend.' or 'I got caught masturbating tonight by my roommate.'

Not all of them were about sex, though. Some were about time in jail, and others about hating their parents. The app was set up so that you could like a post, comment on it, or even message the user of the post privately. Locations were always hidden, and you couldn't send photos or videos in the app—just text.

Sadie settled into her spot and continued reading through the posts, liking a few. When she came across one similar to hers, she commented on one from a user named **RebelsWearLeather**.

The post read, '**I can't stop thinking about her. She's my best friend and yet I search for her in every body that warms the bed beside me in her absence.**"

Sadie felt compelled to write back, a shiver running through her as she started tapping away at her screen.

"I feel these emotions tonight and my heart goes out to you. I am terribly lost in the fantasy of my friendship turning into something more, but he's also a rebel - one without a cause, and he probably thinks I'm too tame."

She smiled at her James Dean reference when she submitted her response, hoping the receiver would appreciate it. Then, she went to get a blanket from the closet to cover herself. She was just situating it over her legs when her phone chimed.

RebelsWearLeather wants to send you a message. Sadie quickly swiped up to reveal a chat screen.

RebelsWearLeather:

> Couldn't help yourself with that one, could you?

Sadie laughed out loud and quickly quieted so as not to wake her boyfriend. Her boyfriend. BOYFRIEND. *Remember him? Get a grip on yourself.*

BookwormBarbie:

> Sorry, you made it too easy. James Dean is a hot topic in my life tonight. If he was a number, I'd buy a lottery ticket.

What am I even saying? Sadie groaned into the blue throw pillow beside her and held her breath until his following message came.

RebelsWearLeather:

> I have to admit I'm intrigued by that. Also, let me extend my apologies to you as well. Seems we're both pining.

BookwormBarbie:

Seems that way. I know better than to ask a stranger where they live, but it's late, and I'm on the East Coast. 4:16 to be exact. Are you up past your bedtime, too?

RebelsWearLeather:

I'm on the East Coast, too. I had a rough night at work and just couldn't settle down. I write in my spare time, and sometimes, I get ideas from the users of this app. Sometimes, I use them as writing prompts.

Sadie's eyebrows rose in response to his last message. *He's smart. A writer. I like those.*

BookwormBarbie:

I love that idea. I just downloaded it tonight actually. You're my first comment.

RebelsWearLeather:

Wow, I'm flattered. I haven't been someone's first in a while.

Sadie chuckled and took a sip of her water. *Is this guy flirting with me?*

BookwormBarbie:

So what are your plans for the rest of the night? Or morning.

RebelsWearLeather:

I'm probably going to make this chick go home, strip the sheets off my bed, and take a shower. I might also try to rest a few hours before I go to work.

Jesus, Sadie thought and rubbed her thighs together, trying to ignore the heat that was pooling between them at his words. *It sounds like he might have had some good sex tonight, at least.*

He sent another text before she could type a response.

RebelsWearLeather:

What about you, Barbie?

BookwormBarbie:

I'm going to get back in bed and hope I can stop thinking of men in leather jackets long enough to finally sleep.

RebelsWearLeather:

Now, why would you want to forget about me already?

He was *definitely* flirting with her.

BookwormBarbie:

Good luck with your houseguest. Hope that works out for you.

RebelsWearLeather:

Doubtful. She didn't want to be tied up, spanked or choked.

Sadie almost dropped her phone, her face burning from the flush across her cheeks. Maybe Travis was right. Maybe she was lying to herself. Perhaps men in leather jackets were her type.

She decided to end the night on a high, choosing to try and flirt back.

BookwormBarbie:

For what it's worth, I would have begged for all three. Goodnight, Rebel.

BookwormBarbie is no longer online.

Sadie exited out of the app and took 3 deep breaths.

No harm was done; it was just some innocent flirting with a man of mystery that got you seriously wet, and you talked to him for all of ten minutes.

She snuck back into Travis's bedroom and under the covers. It was almost dawn. The shrill sounds of birds were gracing her ears as the sun crested the town outside of his windows. She cuddled in closer, taking in his body heat.

She didn't have to go on that app again.

She didn't have to talk to random guys online.

She didn't have to fake orgasms and dodge her boyfriend's advances.

But she was, and she did.

As sleep finally began to calm her, she wondered if there was a way out of the mess inside her head - and her heart.

Chapter FIVE

Jagger hadn't anticipated himself to be taking off Bianca's jacket so soon after putting it on, but seeing Sadie with Travis made him frustrated and tired of pushing off her advances.

When she smashed her lips to his, he took it for what it was worth - a distraction.

He'd led her into the office at the back of the bar and glanced at the private door he usually kept locked at all times. Even Sadie hadn't been allowed back there, telling her it was "just Renegade stuff that needed to be kept hidden." She'd assumed it meant guns or even drugs that had been part of the gig so many years ago before he and his dad had cleaned them up and made the gang into honest men. For the most part, anyway. You can't babysit gang members, after all.

Throughout the past year, Jagger had started to get in touch with a side that had since become a permanent part of him. The dominance in his sexuality allowed him some control over his life that constantly seemed to be falling apart in one area or another. He reveled in the knowledge he gathered, the experiences, and the release that it gave him and started allowing that part of him to indulge in it from time to time in that old storage room and had turned it into a playroom for his more intense sexual encounters.

He wanted to try Bianca out in there, if only to shove a ball gag in her mouth to get her to stop her terrible porn star moans, but he could already tell she was vanilla as shit.

"How would you feel if I tied you up, Bianca?" Jagger asked between open-mouthed kisses and grabbing roughly at her waist.

Bianca laughed. "That's so weird, Mr. Wilder."

This isn't going to work, he thought as she continued to grab at him. So much for letting out his pent-up aggression tonight.

"OOHHH YES!" Bianca was yelling even though he was only kissing her throat, roughly pushing her against the wall in the office and grabbing at the hem of her short black dress. He hoisted the skirt up and rolled his eyes while his mouth pressed against her shoulder, and she cried out again, "OH, MY GOD! TAKE ME!"

"Sure," he grumbled. "But not here, let's go upstairs."

He took one more look behind him at the locked door and led Bianca out of the office and up to his apartment, grabbing her coat off the floor as he made his way behind her.

Let's get this over with, he thought with a grimace. *I can't afford to find another shot girl right now.*

Sometime later, Jagger moved off the bed and pulled his black jeans back over his hips, zipping his fly and buckling up before looking down at the snoring shot girl from the evening's events.

He lit a cigarette and took a deep drag before settling into the black upholstered chair next to his bed, content to take a few minutes before waking Bianca up and getting her out of his place.

He wasn't a monster but women didn't stay over.

Jagger opened up his favorite app, "SecretScape," and began scrolling, liking a few posts for inspiration to use towards the novel he'd been working on since college. A memoir of sorts about how his father had raised him to be a drug mule in high school to help pay for his alcoholism. By the time he was sixteen, he was helping his father's gang bury bodies from their rivals, The Dregs. And by eighteen - well, there was a reason he took off and went to school.

Jagger took another drag and wiped some residual sweat off his brow with the back of his hand, cigarette dangling between his fingertips as he took another look at Bianca's sleeping form. He wanted to pretend it was Sadie lying there and not another random girl. He knew what he was doing wasn't exactly healthy, but there wasn't anything he could do about it right now.

Except...

"Screw it," he muttered out loud and clicked **"Post New Secret"** on the app. He hadn't posted a secret there before, content to indulge in everyone else's, but he felt especially broken tonight.

'I can't stop thinking about her. She's my best friend, and yet I search for her in every body that warms the bed beside me in her absence."

Before he thought better of it, it was posted and joined the other secrets in the tangled web of internet mistakes.

Slipping his phone in his pocket, he held the cigarette between tense lips, grabbed his leather jacket off the floor, and put it over his bare chest. By the time he leaned over to stub it out in the ashtray by his feet next to the bed, it vibrated in his pocket.

When he pulled it out, he grinned at the alert, saying he had a comment on his post from BookwormBarbie. He couldn't help but send her a message responding to the James Dean reference that coincided with his username.

Jagger knew he shouldn't have been so surprised they managed a decent conversation, but he was usually a closed-off individual. However, this was the age of the internet, and if you couldn't talk to strangers about your problems, who could you talk to?

When he sent the message about his bedmate being too dull for him, seeing how far he could push the boundaries, she didn't let him down when she followed up with her own comeback before logging off.

Beg, huh? Jagger thought with a slow grin. He felt himself harden in his jeans and let out a low curse before looking over at Bianca.

"Nope. Not making that mistake again."

Jagger went downstairs to the bar, his head pounding from lack of sleep and the sound system's bass traveling through his floorboards.

"Sadie!" He called out, "You here?!"

Jagger was still in the dark gray sweatpants he changed into after he came in from walking Bianca out to her Uber during the night, his chest bare. He leaned over the staircase's banister and looked towards the bar area but saw no one. Only Sadie and Warren, his dad, had keys to the bar, and he knew he locked that shit up tight after Bianca left in case she tried to come back unannounced.

Jagger opened his mouth to yell again, a wave of panic rising in his chest, and he began to clock where he'd hidden the guns around the bar last year. As his eyes drifted towards the stage at the other end of the bar, he clenched his fists and tried to relax because Sadie was currently moving around the pole in a flash of black fabric against creamy white skin. He hadn't realized how long her hair had gotten since they finished college, but it had been a while since she stopped cutting it.

Jagger couldn't help but notice now as it whipped against the top of her ass when she threw her head back.

He swallowed hard and had to force his fists to unclench. He almost felt bad for watching her.

Almost.

Sadie hadn't noticed him over the music, obviously lost in her movements, sweat glistening on her skin and causing what little clothes she had on to stick to her. Jagger's eyes never left the lines of her body as he made his way to the bottom of the stairs and leaned his bare shoulder against the wall. He took in how well she moved in time to the song playing, vaguely catching some of the pretty dirty lyrics. His lips pulled up in a smirk, finally recognizing '*Backstage*' by NEFFEX.

Sadie always had the most interesting taste in music, her playlists consisting of show tunes, pop ballads, and songs you'd typically hear in a strip club.

He loved that about her.

Suddenly, he felt the too-familiar rush of lust for his friend. His headache was soon replaced by another ache in his cock as it twitched in response to the vision in front of him.

Sadie slid her hands up the pole and lifted herself up, keeping her legs straight as she swung them to hook her ankles together and caught the pole tightly between the apex of her thighs. She slowly leaned backward, her fingers tracing the pole, and then they were gliding up her chest, and a hand gripped her throat as she tossed her head back. Her eyes were closed, and her hands were now tangling in her hair, the black bralette top she wore straining against her breasts that threatened to spill from her movements.

Jagger wished more than anything to feel those fucking legs wrapped around his neck, licking her through the lacy scrap of fabric that was hugging that perfect mound of flesh. He wanted to hear her whimpers and make her lose control. He wanted to replace her hands with his and grip her golden locks in his fists as he forced her to look at him when he forced himself inside her. He wanted to-

His fantasies were interrupted as he watched her eyes open and lock with his, still upside down on the pole.

Sadie's breath caught in her throat, and she quickly reached above her to grab the pole and start getting down. Within a few moments, she was right-side up, her legs releasing to bring her feet down to the ground. She ran to the edge of the stage and shut the song off with a quick button. The stereo system that her phone was plugged into was still glowing.

"I'm *so* sorry! Did I wake you?" Sadie asked as she quickly stepped into her motorcycle boots, which remained unlaced. She made her way down the few steps of the stage to meet him on the main floor. She'd been bartending long enough to know better than to walk barefoot throughout the bar, brushing off how little she was wearing. He'd seen her in bathing suits before, and during the summers, they'd managed to sneak away to the shore for a day. But in this environment, it was different.

Jagger didn't realize he'd been walking toward her since she shut the music off until they stood toe-to-toe. He let his eyes wander down her body, and when he looked back into her doe eyes that had the nerve to look so innocently at him while the body in front of him was a picture of sin, he thought he'd died and gone to hell. Her face was flushed from her physical activity, and Jagger wanted nothing more than to wrap his long fingers around her neck and pull her in for a hard kiss. Instead, he cleared his throat and said, "I thought you were going to do this at night."

Sadie's eyebrows drew together as she gave him a look. "I'm sorry you were still sleeping, Jag. It's past eleven; I figured you'd be awake by now. The bar is opening in 10 minutes," she said as if that explained everything.

Despite his best efforts, Jagger couldn't stop darting his eyes across her chest and torso. He blamed it on still being half-asleep but deep down he knew it was a bald-faced fucking lie.

Sadie tried to cover herself better and pulled at the fabric of her black bralette that clung to her ribs, hoping it would magically get long enough to conceal her torso.

Jagger's expression did nothing to hide his amusement at how nervous she suddenly looked, seeming as though she finally understood she was standing in the middle of the bar in little more than her underwear and boots.

God, those fucking boots.

She might as well be wearing high heels with how they affected him right now.

"I didn't sleep well last night," he admitted. "But, I have to say, it's not the worst way to wake up, Sweets." He was clearly teasing her and raised an eyebrow at her discomfort.

Sadie ran her small, manicured hands over her face and groaned. "You're lucky I love it when you call me that."

She wrapped her arms around herself in a hug and tried not to feel self-conscious when she realized what she admitted. Sadly, in doing so, she missed the searing look on his face.

"I normally would have stayed after, but Travis borrowed my car and I needed him to pick me up, and you and Bianca seemed to be cozy, so I felt it best to just head home."

Jagger scoffed at the mention of Bianca and hooked a thumb in the waistband of his sweatpants to rest his hand in an imaginary pocket. The slight movement drew them down enough to show the curve of his tanned hip bone and a snake tattoo she had thought about on more than one occasion. Sadie had never seen the entire piece but had imagined it must have gone down his thigh the way it coiled over the top of the slight V that trailed downwards.

Sadie's brows furrowed, and her tongue darted to wet her lips. "What's wrong with Bianca? She's beautiful. All legs and flaming red hair."

Jagger laughed out loud, the sound echoing in the empty bar.

"She's definitely something," he said with dripping sarcasm.

They were still standing so close to one another that Sadie tried to lie to herself when she attributed her shallow breathing to her morning workout. She came to work off some of the sexual tension she was feeling from not one but three men. Honestly, her soul couldn't take much more of this. She needed a better boyfriend, a better lay, and a goddamn orgasm.

They stood in a silent game of chicken for what felt like an eternity. Neither of them moved closer, but they did not move away from one another, either.

Sadie surprised herself when her hand reached out to toy with the un-tied drawstrings hanging from his waistband, brushing against his hand with her own. Jagger stood utterly still and fought the desire to pull her to him. His blue eyes shone in the bar's lights as he looked down at her small frame. The entire scenario was sending a rush of blood to his cock, and the bulge in his pants started to be painfully evident through his sweatpants since he wasn't wearing anything underneath.

It might be possible to control his breathing, but he couldn't control *that.*

She brought her other hand to the front of his waist-line, and her fingertips grazed against the hard length, shielded only by thin cotton as she worked up the nerve to run her fingers along his waistline. When she reached the tattooed snake, her fingers traced the tail and down the length of its torso. His skin was so hot against her fingertips that she was ghosting her hand over his to grip the waistband before she realized it.

"Sadie," Jagger breathed, halting her movements and putting his hand over hers. Just as her eyes flitted up to meet his, there was a sharp knock at the door.

"Come on, it's 11:32!" A gruff voice called, causing Sadie to jump and yank her hands back to her sides. "Ya'll should've been open two minutes ago!"

Sadie tried to look anywhere except at Jagger's face. She was so thoroughly embarrassed by her recent actions. Might as well be throwing herself at him at this point. Time to get her damn libido in check.

"I-I, I should change." She stammered and made her way behind the bar, where her bag was hidden from plain sight. She pulled out a change of clothes and willed herself not to turn around, sensing Jagger's eyes on her.

Why isn't he moving? She thought. *You really fucked this one up. Just because you're horny doesn't mean you have to assault Jagger. What's wrong with you?*

Sadie heard him moving as she quickly pulled her white Serpent Pit shirt over her head, his words coming shortly after.

"I'm going to change, too. Unlock the front door when you're covered," he spoke quietly, his voice strained.

Sadie tugged her black leggings up over her hips and threw an "Okay!" over her shoulder, her attention now on pulling on her boots. The gruffness of his voice did not go unnoticed by her, and her hands shook as she struggled to tie the laces.

"Oh, and Sadie?" Jagger questioned from the top of the staircase, hesitating before he reached his apartment door. His eyes met hers as she looked up from tying her boots, finally meeting his gaze.

"I enjoyed your performance." His gaze moved from the stage back to her once more. "Feel free to interrupt my sleep anytime."

And with that, he was through the door to his apartment, leaving Sadie with her mouth hanging open and her body thrumming with something very close to desire.

Chapter FIVE

Sadie was exhausted. She and Jagger had been managing the bar all day and were stuck there until closing time. It was Saturday, their busiest night of the week, and she was thankful when Bianca and Camille came in to deal with the crowd by eight. Bianca was handing out shots like glasses of water, Camille was helping Sadie behind the bar, and Jagger was walking the space with Gremlin, keeping an eye on the patrons.

The whole day was filled with tension, and Jagger and Sadie barely spoke, choosing to keep themselves busy cleaning up after customers or changing taps. It wasn't until the end of the night when Bianca decided to pull her shit again, that Sadie realized how on edge she was from it all.

"Bianca, can you bring these beers over to the gentlemen by the pool table when you head back to the floor?" Sadie asked, handing her a newly filled tray of shots. With

Jagger not behind the bar, Bianca was forced to limit her interactions with him, leaving Sadie to help her throughout the night.

Bianca rolled her eyes as she replied, "Run your own beers, bitch."

"Excuse me?" Sadie's eyebrows shot up, and she turned to look at her.

"You heard me," she sneered at her. "Besides, I'm with Jagger now. I don't gotta do shit for you."

Sadie slammed the tray on the counter, coming from behind the bar to meet her. The bar was so loud that most didn't hear the commotion or see the whiskey pouring over the bartop onto the floor from the toppled glasses. Camille signaled over to Jagger and Gremlin when she sensed that things were about to get heated between the girls. It was only confirmed when Sadie snarled, "What the fuck are you talking about, Bianca?"

Bianca crossed her arms, pushing her breasts up in the tiny black dress she always wore, looking the part of the pathetic skank everyone knew her to be.

"*Fuck* being the operative word." She said smugly, "You didn't think I went home after you left, did you? Someone has to keep up with that man, and we all know you're too boring to do it."

Sadie tried to process the feeling of hurt that flooded her senses, flashes of their moment that morning clouding her judgment. She blamed it on that when she pulled back and punched Bianca right in the face, not caring how her hand screamed in pain afterward.

"What the FUCK?!" Bianca screamed as she clutched her hands over her face, blood pouring from her nose.

At this point, the sounds of *Sleep Token* could only cover so much, and several customers within hearing distance turned to survey the scene unraveling in front of them. Jagger was there instantly, having rushed ahead of Gremlin to get to Sadie.

"What's going on here?!" He roared, pushing past the last few customers to get to the girls.

Bianca turned to him and started crying, turning the waterworks on full blast, "That bitch!" She pointed at Sadie and tried to clutch the front of his jacket, but he pushed her off. "Look what she did!"

Camille tossed her short pink hair up into a messy bun in case she had to get involved herself when she saw Sadie fisting her hands at her sides. She turned towards Sadie and grabbed her attention, forcing her to look at her. "Go cool off, I'll handle this."

Sadie said nothing, just nodded at her before brushing past Jagger and Bianca, making sure to body-check her with a sharp elbow as she did.

Bianca lunged at Sadie, and Jagger grabbed her by the shoulders and forced her to look at him, not bothering to be gentle.

"Explain. Now. What did you say to her?"

Camille and Gremlin were already thinning out the crowd and distracting them from the fight. Thankfully, the girls dancing on stage had most of the bar busy. "Next rounds on the house, guys! Get them in before the last call!"

Bianca grabbed some napkins from the bar and pressed them to her nose. "I didn't do anything. I just told her we were together," she pouted through her crocodile tears.

Jagger barely resisted the urge to throttle her, but he couldn't control how his grip tightened considerably around her shoulders. "You what?" he growled, noticing her nose was off-center and feeling proud that Sadie had clearly broken it.

Bianca winced at the pain, "She's awful! I told her that now we're together, and she needs to understand I'm with you and get it through her head that I don't have to take orders from her here."

Jagger released her then, afraid he'd break her arms at this point. "Bianca. We fucked. We're not dating," he explained slowly. "And honestly, it was a goddamn chore to keep my cock hard enough to screw you last night."

Bianca's eyes widened in shock as she sputtered, "W-what?!"

Jagger raised a hand up and gestured over her head to the person behind her. "Clean her up, pay her, and get her out of here."

Gremlin, who had stayed close by in case he was needed, started getting Bianca's things from behind the bar.

"You disrespect me when you disrespect Sadie," he said calmly as he turned his attention back to Bianca, although his eyes were almost blown black with anger.

"Don't ever step foot in here again."

Sadie found herself in the walk-in freezer, unbothered by the cold temperature. She was seething as she paced back and forth, the thoughts in her head taunting her.

I can't believe it! she thought, even though she had no fundamental right to be mad. She wasn't his, and he wasn't hers. They were good friends, that was true—best friends. But recently, things have been different. How he talked to her and how his eyes took her in when she came in for her shifts now. And she hadn't been all that innocent in that regard because she was purposefully wearing more revealing outfits at the bar.

She was trying to catch his attention, secretly hoping to see if he had any interest in her as more than a friend. Camille offered to cut up her Serpent Pit t-shirts they were supposed to wear at work, and Sadie was grateful, loving how it complimented her and made her feel edgy, a far cry from her pastel attire when working with her mom. She loved how she somehow fit into this world, grateful for her time there and how she could escape her 'perfect' life that lay outside the smoke-filled bar.

She hadn't known how much he would affect her in turn. His body had changed, his arms thicker from working out at the gym in town. She felt different around him as if she were crawling out of her skin. It was lightyears away from the comfortable friendship they had cultivated for years. And something had to give soon.

They couldn't go on like this.

Sadie knew she was being unreasonable, but Bianca deserved to get punched in the face for mouthing off.

Tripping over one of the boxes of Stella Artois on the floor, she felt another wave of animosity rise in her. She yelled, "I hope I broke her fucking nose!" then, unsuccessfully, tried to kick a hole in the metal wall of the back of the freezer, unaware that the freezer door had opened behind her.

"I'm pretty sure you did," Jagger said from the threshold, stepping inside to join her, the door closing softly behind him.

Sadie turned around and folded her arms across her chest.

"Good. She still here?"

Jagger shook his head, his dark locks falling over his forehead.

"I'm not apologizing to your girlfriend," Sadie seethed, and her voice was colder than the temperature around them.

"You didn't do anything wrong," Jagger said softly. "She's not - "

Sadie tried to push past him, her blood still boiling from the altercation with Bianca. "Save it, Jag."

Within seconds, she found her back pressed against one of the metal racks, gasping at the feel of ice-cold steel against her bare lower back under her crop top. Jagger had grasped her wrists in his hands when he shouted, "Goddamn it, Sadie! Just fucking listen to me for a minute."

Her back had arched of its own volition, trying to escape the burning sensation of the metal on her skin. It was causing her breasts to press hard against his chest, and she wondered if that feeling didn't burn through her twice as much.

He continued when she finally stopped struggling against him, "Bianca is nothing to me. Not a girlfriend. Honestly, not even someone I care to be in the same room with."

Sadie finally lifted her eyes to his.

"But she said -"

"I know what she said, Sweets. I just fired her. Did I sleep with her? Yes. Was it terrible? Yes. I couldn't wait to kick her out afterward," he admitted, and Sadie felt herself laugh at that. The movement of her mirth caused her chest to brush against his even more, and she let out a sudden moan at the sensation.

Jagger felt her hardened nipples through both of their shirts, the feeling spiking his arousal instantly, and her moan was his breaking point. Without thinking, he pressed his face into her neck and inhaled her scent, his fingers releasing her wrists before running along her fore-arms and settling on her hips. Sadie whimpered quietly and took that moment to grip his biceps, feeling their strength beneath her fingertips even through the leather of his jacket.

Feeling his hot breath against her neck, she knew in her soul that the goosebumps covering her body were from him and not from the cold.

Jagger's tongue swiped along the pulse in her throat, and she cried out, clutching at the sleeves of his jacket. Her pussy was throbbing against his jean-wrapped thigh that was now pressing between her legs to balance them both. Neither knew what the hell had come over them, but they were melting despite the frigid contents of their frozen little world. Jagger took his time kissing up the length of her neck and nibbling at her jawline before his large hand moved to grasp her throat, his silver rings biting into the flesh and tilting her face toward him. The sound she made in response shook his resolve even further, and when she stared up at him and parted her lips, he was done for. Boyfriend be damned.

"Sadie! Jag! Where are you guys?!" they vaguely heard through the door.

Jagger stepped backward, putting a good three feet between them, and stared at her flushed face. Her lips quivered as she panted, little clouds forming from the cold as the hot breath escaped her mouth.

Camille swung open the freezer door and remarked, "What the hell are you guys doing in here? Trying to freeze to death?!"

They still hadn't taken their eyes off one another, and Sadie and Jagger both had the same thought run through their minds—*they were burning*.

"We got everyone cleared out, and Bianca is long gone," she informed them as she held the door open wide in a gesture for them to step out, shivering a bit from the rush of cold blowing towards her. "Come on, Sadie. I'll drive you home. You had a rough night."

Sadie was the first to look away, smiling at Camille and leaving the freezer. "Thanks," she said as she passed by.

Jagger's expression was far less friendly, giving Camille a frustrated glare. Camille had been one of his closest friends since they were children, and she had lived this gang life for just as long as he had. There were a few occasions when their fathers tried to set them up, but Jagger had always known Camille had a thirst for vodka, Sour Patch Kids, and, well... women.

"What?!" Camille asked incredulously, her pink hair falling over her shoulder as she tilted her head to shake out the messy bun from before.

"Nothing," Jagger said, leaving the freezer and going up to his apartment.

Camille stood staring at the cooler momentarily before her brain caught up with the situation unfolding around her.

"Oh," she said to herself, nervously running her hand through her hair. "*Oh*. I get it now."

Chapter SIX

Sadie was grateful to be back at her apartment tonight. With a quick text to Travis to let him know she was home from work safe, she allowed herself to finally breathe. She stripped out of her work clothes, leaving her in the sporty underwear she wore that morning at the bar when she was on the pole. Her room had always been comforting with its lavender walls and black furniture. Feminine yet still a touch of darkness like the kind she so often longed to give herself over to.

Collapsing onto the plush white comforter on her bed, Sadie found herself frustrated beyond belief. The aching between her legs continued to grow with no relief in sight, and she couldn't help but think of how the night had taken a turn. She thought of Jagger and how his calloused hand felt on her throat and how hot his mouth was on her skin.

The muffled scream she tried to drown in her pillow still bounced off the walls around her.

Sadie raised her phone to her face and anxiously scrolled through her apps, looking for her target. She clicked on it, searched for the message section, and bit her lip.

The green dot icon next to **RebelsWearLeather** meant he was online.

She clutched her phone nervously before making the decision to message him. She was not about to message Jagger after tonight had left her in a puddle of mixed emotions and pent-up sexual angst.

But this guy might be her ticket to a safe fantasy.

She could pretend he was Jagger for a night to help get her off, right?

BookwormBarbie:

> Have you ever masturbated with a stranger before?

Jagger was enjoying a smoke in his favorite chair next to his bed again, his cock still painfully hard from having Sadie pressed against him in the freezer. He was scrolling through his phone, trying to take his mind off of her so he could think clearly, when he received a message.

"Oh, Jesus," he mumbled and sank back into the chair, letting his legs stretch out before him. The smoke from his cigarette casting a shadow on his already cloudy mood.

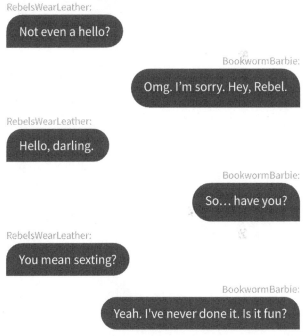

RebelsWearLeather:

Not even a hello?

BookwormBarbie:

Omg. I'm sorry. Hey, Rebel.

RebelsWearLeather:

Hello, darling.

BookwormBarbie:

So… have you?

RebelsWearLeather:

You mean sexting?

BookwormBarbie:

Yeah. I've never done it. Is it fun?

Jagger let out a pained laugh, realizing he would have to jerk off before getting any kind of sleep at this point. These women were ruining him from all angles.

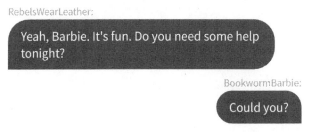

RebelsWearLeather:

Yeah, Barbie. It's fun. Do you need some help tonight?

BookwormBarbie:

Could you?

RebelsWearLeather:

> Yeah, sure. Why not?

Jagger put his cigarette out in the ashtray and let out one last cloud of smoke before pulling his jeans and gray boxer briefs off and getting into bed.

Holding the phone in his left hand, he used the right one to wrap around his cock, slowly pumping up and down. He texted deftly with just one hand, having learned how to handle scrolling through porn with one hand and jerking off with the other in his teens.

He let himself think of Sadie and put her face on this stranger as he messaged her in detail about what he would do to her if he were there. In this way, he was explaining everything he wished he could be doing to Sadie right now. And that would have to be enough.

For now.

Sadie lay stretched out on her bed, legs spread wide, and knees slightly bent. Ever so eager, she awaited instruction on what to do.

Sadie quickly typed another "Yes" in response and slipped her hand inside the top of her black panties. She imagined how Jagger had looked at her in these that morning, how wet he had made her then. She glided around her clit with ease, the wetness coating her fingers.

RebelsWearLeather:

> I want you to imagine my cock teasing your pussy, how good it would feel to slip inside you. I'd rub the tip against that clit until you whimpered for me. I'd take you slow at first until you were begging for me to go harder and wrap my hand around your throat. I want to leave you breathless in all sense of the word. You told me you would beg for it, didn't you?

Sadie moaned, already feeling the sensation of an impending orgasm building. She struggled to type back but still managed to do so quickly.

BookwormBarbie:

> I would. I want you to ruin my pussy. I want you to flip me over, take me from behind, and pull my hair.

RebelsWearLeather:

> Fuck. That's it, darling. I'm so close. You're such a good girl for me. I want you to get yourself to the edge, and when you're about to cum, I need you to put two fingers inside your pussy while you continue to work your clit.

Sadie listened and continued to furiously move her fingertips against her clit, arching off the bed. She pictured Jagger in her mind's eye, shirtless and beautiful. She imagined the feeling of him against her earlier, wishing Camille had never interrupted, content to have frozen to death in that freezer if it meant him being inside her.

When she felt herself start to lose control, she grabbed her phone again, wanting her stranger to finish with her.

> BookwormBarbie:
> I'm right there. I'm going to soak my bed for you.

> BookwormBarbie:
> Will you spill yourself all over your hand for me? Please.

Sadie kept an intense eye on her screen. When she saw his next message, she dropped her phone on the bed beside her and shoved her fingers inside, the extra pressure sending her straight over the edge.

> RebelsWearLeather:
> Sweets Jesus, I'm coming for you. Fuck.

Sadie's pussy convulsed around her fingers, letting herself fully immerse herself in the fantasy that she was doing this with Jagger. The mystery man's typo of saying Sweets instead of Sweet was everything she needed, although she knew he probably struggled to type while getting off with her. Whatever the reason, she was grateful for it.

She finally had a release.

For the time being, at least.

Jagger tossed his phone on the nightstand and reached for the tissues beside it. He swiped them over his right hand and wiped his cock clean of the evidence of his orgasm.

I can't believe I fucking slipped up and let it auto-correct to Sweets, he thought as he tossed them in the trashcan in the corner of his room. He knew she didn't understand the connotation behind it, but seeing it typed out made the fantasy all too real for him.

Easy mistake.

He slid into his bed naked and gazed out of the large studio windows where rain started to pelt. He hoped he could talk with Sadie before they opened the bar again the next day. At least it was a small shift since it was Sunday. Just the lunch crowd, and they could close up after. She had evidently felt just as turned on as he did tonight. He knew he didn't make it up.

Maybe, just maybe, she would be open to being some-thing more. Jagger knew he would take anything he could get with Sadie at this point. She could tell him to lick those damn motorcycle boots, and he would do it with a smile on his face.

As he ran a hand through his hair and thought about approaching the subject with her, he reached for his phone. The light illuminated the concentrated expression on his face as he sent one more message to the girl from tonight. She seemed like an innocent little thing, and her sexting could use a little work, but she wanted to be bad. He liked that about her because it reminded him of his Sadie—*his Sadie*.

Christ, he was so gone for her it was ridiculous.

RebelsWearLeather:

> I hope you had "fun" tonight. I know I did.
> Goodnight, darling.

He sucked in his breath and sat up abruptly when he read her incoming message, remembering those exact words affecting him earlier that day in the dimly lit bar.

BookwormBarbie:

> I did. I like it when you call me that.

Son of a bitch, Jagger began to wonder.

Just as he went to set his phone down, it started ringing.

"What now?" he barked into the receiver after seeing who was calling him.

"Is that any way to speak to your old man, boy?" the voice answered, crackling through the silence.

Jagger sat up and leaned his back against the iron headboard. "Yeah, it's pretty valid, considering you've been gone for two years now and only call to have me clean up your messes."

"Our messes."

"Your messes," Jagger hissed through the phone and angrily threw the covers off himself to begin dressing. "I've made the Serpent Pit a decent place while you've been gone. And the Renegade Rebels have been staying out of trouble. I don't need you to constantly stir up more bullshit from across the fucking states."

There was a pause before Warren spoke. "Listen, I know you want out, but this lifestyle doesn't just go away. Especially with The Dregs around, okay?"

"I am excruciatingly aware of that."

"Good. So, you know why I need a favor."

Jagger pulled the phone away from his ear long enough to throw a long-sleeved black shirt on. "Fucking hell."

"Listen, The Dregs have been peddling drugs to the kids around town. There have been several deaths just this past week. Now, I know this isn't a usual call, but-"

Jagger cut him off as he finished pulling his jeans and boots on. "Oh, so I'm not burying bodies tonight?"

"Not if you don't want to, you little shit!" Warren yelled into the phone, and Jagger stalked out of his apartment. He was already on his way to the old red '98 Ford truck he used for situations like this, grabbing his jacket.

"Now, pay attention. They have a shack located off the highway about thirty meters into the woods right outside the city. I need you to return it to the bar and hide it in my office. I will try to come back soon and get rid of it. They won't have enough connections to get another shipment that big for a while, and until I find who they're getting this shit from, we need to cut them off at their knees while we can."

"Don't worry about coming back, I'll get rid of it tonight."

"And how are you going to do that?"

Jagger turned over the engine and grabbed a cigarette from his pocket before answering, "I learned a lot over the years, pop. You taught me how to deal, kill, destroy and hide. You think I can just forget?"

There was a pause.

"Make sure to grab some backup from the warehouse; Gremlin should be there to help."

"Already on my way."

Another long pause.

"Don't do anything stupid, boy. But if you have to," Warren let out a low chuckle. "Hide some bodies."

Chapter SEVEN

Sadie had plans to meet with Travis at the local coffee shop near the Serpent Pit the following day. She was getting nervous and shuffled around in her seat a little while she took a sip from her second cup of coffee. He had texted her he would be late, but she didn't think he meant THIS late.

She spent the last hour in the corner, sitting on an uncomfortable wicker chair by the window, going over the events from the previous couple of days, wondering about the repercussions she would face. And then there was the 'Secret' stranger she had met online.

Sadie crossed her legs tightly to alleviate some of the tension her memories inflicted. She tried desperately not to recall Jagger's hard body pressed to hers the night before and the evidence of his lust barely concealed by his sweatpants at seeing her yesterday morning. Instead, she checked her phone to see what time it was. It was already 10:18am.

Shit, Sadie thought as she rested the side of her head against the glass of the window beside her and looked out at the main road leading towards the wrong part of town.

I wanted to get there early enough to talk to Jag before we opened.

As she had that thought, the roar of a motorcycle sounded in the distance. She picked her head up and turned slightly so her full attention was on the road, the view a little hazy as she looked past her own reflection in the window. In less than five seconds, Jagger was pulling into the coffee shop's parking lot on his all-black bike.

"Oh, my god," Sadie started to panic, smoothing her hands down her black jeans to wipe the sweat that had quickly begun to pull from her palms. She had on another black and neon Serpent Pit crop top that Camille insisted looked better on her than should be allowed and an old Renegade Rebels jacket that Jagger had given her in college when he got too built to wear it any longer swung over the back of her chair. She barely resisted the urge to throw it over her head and hide.

She sank into her seat and watched him from the window as he took off his helmet and looked up.

Holding her breath, Sadie watched him toss his hair out of his eyes as he lifted a hand in greeting. She exhaled shakily and lifted a slight wave in his direction, which was rewarded with a wide grin as he made his way to the front door. Once inside, he went to the counter and got a coffee and breakfast sandwich before sitting in the seat across from her.

"Hi," Sadie mumbled, taking another sip of her coffee, a super sweet concoction with milk and caramel flavoring. At least she was grateful that her hands had something to keep them busy other than reaching out and grabbing at him like a cat in heat.

"Hey, Sweets," Jagger said and took in her appearance.

She really shouldn't look that sexy this early, his internal self mused. Sadie's eyes flashed with something he couldn't quite place, but he hoped it was a realization.

She let out something between a cough and a laugh, thinking of how far gone she was when thinking about him last night with the stranger.

"What?" He asked, his fingertips grazing her knee under the table. She could feel the heat from his hand through her jeans instantly. "Are you okay? I thought you said you liked it when I called you that."

Sadie nodded quickly and looked away from him. "So, what are you doing here? You have coffee at your place."

Then, Jagger bit into his breakfast sandwich, and with an exaggerated moan, he said, "But I don't have this delicious food there." He took another bite, already halfway done with how quickly he inhaled his food. "I should have gone grocery shopping the other day, but this week has left me..." He paused, and his eyes were way too intense for this coffee shop setting when he looked at her. "Distracted."

One of the workers came by and asked if they needed anything, causing Sadie to almost jump out of her skin. "No, we're good!" she chirped, her tone friendly.

"So what are you doing here by yourself, Sweets? And how'd you get here this morning if your car is still parked at the bar?" He used her nickname again, but she was more prepared this time.

"I took an Uber since I was supposed to meet with Travis here before my shift, but I don't know where he is. I know he had some pre-game meeting with the others, but he said he needed to talk, so I dragged myself here when I could have stayed in bed a little longer," she said in a huff and folded her arms across her chest.

Jagger put down his coffee while she elaborated on her morning and grinned, "It's always nice staying in bed."

Sadie rolled her eyes. "That's what you took away from that, huh? And why are you so flirty lately?" She asked before she could help herself.

Jagger broke out into a laugh. "My best friend isn't giving me much of a chance to be anything but that. Did you forget it's Sunday? You're dressed like it's Saturday night and you're trying to make rent in one shift."

Sadie flipped him off, her powder pink nails contrasting her attire, and he laughed again.

"At least I showed up this morning so you don't have to walk or take another Uber now," he smirked.

"You'll give me a ride?" She asked before her mind caught up with her mouth.

Jagger leaned forward, the sound of his leather jacket - a matching set with hers - creaking as his forearms rested on the table. He had given her that jacket as protection. So everyone knew she belonged to him. To the Renegade Rebels, anyway.

"You can take a ride anytime, darling."

Sadie visibly gulped and Jagger winked at her as he sat back in his chair when suddenly her phone rang, and she was thankful for the interruption.

It was Travis. *Finally.*

She pressed the green accept button and said, "Travis? Where are you? It's been an hour now. Should—" Sadie paused, and her eyebrows shot together in concentration.

Jagger looked at her and mouthed, "Everything okay?"

Sadie nodded at Jagger and spoke into the phone again, "Hello?"

What is that? She thought, listening to the weird sounds against her ear. She looked at Jagger again and held her hand over the speaker part of the phone so as not to be heard.

"I think I hear voices," she whispered-shouted across from him.

Jagger reached over and grabbed the phone from Sadie's ear before she could protest what he would do. He hit the speakerphone button and placed it on the table between them, both leaning their ears towards it. There was shuffling and what sounded like crying. Then a loud bang, and what sounded like a woman giggling.

Jagger realized what was happening before Sadie did and reached for her phone to end the call. He wasn't fast enough, though, because she snatched it before he could touch it and listened intently.

She didn't realize he was trying to keep her from being hurt. But when Sadie heard the loud moaning of Travis's name by whoever was with him, and she gradually realized that they were having sex, she didn't have that reaction. No, not at all.

She started laughing.

When Jagger tilted his head to the side and stared at her like she had lost it, it only made her amusement flow harder. Relief flooded her body, and she realized that her and Travis were both interested in other people and that this breakup could happen easily.

"Have fun!" Sadie yelled at the phone, drawing the eyes of the other patrons in the shop.

Sadie didn't think he could hear her, but almost immediately, she heard the rustle of fabric and then, "Sadie? Sadie?! Oh, shit - "

Jagger finally succeeded in grabbing the phone a second time and ended the call as Travis realized he'd been caught.

"You okay?" He asked and slid her phone across the small table back to her.

She smiled and nodded her head. "Yeah, I am. Honestly, it's a good thing. We weren't working, and I've felt that way for a while."

Sadie slid the phone into her jacket pocket behind her as Travis's name began flashing on her screen. "Looks like he feels the same way now, too."

Jagger sat back in his chair and threaded his hands behind his head. Sadie dropped her eyes to the table so as not to look at his biceps flexing through his jacket. "At least you guys didn't move in together. Didn't he ask you a few months back?"

Sadie shuddered at the memory. "Yeah, but I could never be with him that much. He was so perfect and made me feel like I was always walking on eggshells."

"I remember you being pretty perfect when we met," Jagger snorted. "You still are to most people; I just know you better."

Sadie's face softened. "Yeah, you know me better than anyone else, Jag."

They stared at each other, the outside world fading away as they were filled with a multifaceted understanding.

Sadie was the one who broke the tension first, rising from her seat. "Well, that's it then. Glad I didn't have to continue sleeping with him," she said while slipping her jacket on. "Not that it was horrible, but it was... was..." She buried her face in her hands and groaned. "Ugh, I sound like such an asshole."

"Vanilla?" Jagger grinned, standing with her and picking their coffees off the table.

Sadie nodded. "Yeah, it was so boring. I'm not some delicate flower. Sometimes I just want it a little rough, you know?"

Sadie missed this.

Especially the way that they used to be open enough to talk about things like this.

A wicked smile played on Jagger's lips as he disposed of the garbage on their way out to the parking lot. "I'll keep that in mind, Sweets."

Sadie eyed Jagger's motorcycle hesitantly as they walked through the parking lot. She hadn't ridden on the back of it in years, not since they were in college together.

"Come on, it'll be fun," Jagger said, nudging her playfully. "Just like old times."

Sadie shook her head. "I don't know...I like my car. It's safe and reliable." She thought about her old white Porsche which was safely parked at The Serpent Pit waiting for her. Jagger had fixed it up for her when they first moved here since he knew she needed something to get around town in. The car had been abandoned in the back of the Serpent Pit, likely stolen at some point.

Or at least that's what Sadie always assumed but she knew better than to ask questions she didn't want the answers to.

"Yeah, but nothing beats the freedom of riding," Jagger argued. He took his helmet off the bike and turned to Sadie.

"Here, let me get this on you properly."

He stepped closer and gently guided the helmet onto her head. His fingers brushed against her neck as he adjusted the strap, sending a shiver down her spine. Sadie held her breath, suddenly very aware of his proximity and she failed not to think about the night before.

Jagger's hands lingered, playing with her long hair before draping it carefully over her shoulders.

"There. A perfect fit," he murmured, his voice low.

Sadie swallowed hard as his eyes bored into hers. He was so close she could feel the heat radiating off his body. Again. Fuck.

They were too close.

Jagger leaned in slightly, his breath tickling her ear. "Come on, Sweets. Live a little."

His words were both a dare and a plea. Sadie hesitated only a moment longer before nodding.

"Okay, fine. But go slow, okay?"

Jagger's face lit up in a dazzling smile. "You got it."

He straddled the bike and Sadie climbed on behind him, wrapping her arms around his muscular torso. Her heart pounded as she pressed against his back, flooded with memories.

Jagger revved the engine and sped out of the parking lot. Sadie clung to him tightly, equal parts exhilarated and terrified. She had forgotten how good this felt, how safe she always felt with him.

The roar of Jagger's motorcycle filled Sadie's ears as they sped down the winding road toward town. As they rounded a sharp bend, Jagger's hand instinctively reached back and gripped Sadie's thigh, his fingers digging into her flesh through her jeans.

A surprised moan escaped Sadie's lips at the sudden contact, her body tensing against his. Jagger's grip tightened in response, his hand remaining firmly in place as they continued their ride. Heat radiated from his touch, igniting a fire within Sadie that she couldn't ignore as it found a home for itself right in her core.

Embarrassment flooded through her as she realized the intimacy of their position was causing her body to react against her better morals. She tried to focus on the scenery rushing by, but her mind kept drifting back to the feel of Jagger's strong hand on her thigh. When the vibrations from the engine tickled the apex of her thighs and stimulated her clit, she couldn't help grinding herself on the seat behind him to relieve the tension.

Jagger's hand moved down to grasp her calf and pulled her further down the seat until her pelvis was pressed to his hips, eliciting another moan behind him. It took all the power in the world for him not to wipe out on the road with her so obviously trying to get off behind him.

Just as she was about to finish, she saw the lights of The Serpent Pit come into view and the bike slowed down along with its vibrations, leaving Sadie soaked and frustrated.

As they pulled into the parking lot, Jagger reluctantly released his hold on Sadie's leg. She immediately dismounted the bike, mumbling a quick "thank you" as she handed him the helmet. Jagger took it from her and opened his mouth to speak but she practically jumped backwards before rushing inside the bar, desperate to escape the intensity of the moment.

Jagger watched as Sadie disappeared through the door, his heart racing from more than just the ride. He stood alone in the parking lot, his mind replaying the feel of her body pressed against his, the sound of her moans still echoing in his ears. Glancing down at the leather seat where she was perched just a moment ago, he noticed a slight wetness glisten in the sunlight.

And he did what he never thought he'd be desperate enough to do.

He leaned down and ran his tongue along it.

They had made it to the bar with a mere five minutes to spare and opened it to the patrons. Jagger had just poured the first round of drinks out to the customers when someone grumbled about it being too quiet in there.

"I'll fix it! Sorry, guys!" Sadie apologized, went to the sound system and plugged her phone in. She normally used her phone to play music when she worked during the day and the DJ wasn't here, but she had forgotten about it while getting the bar opened a little late with Jagger.

She swiped through her phone until she settled on her favorite playlist instead of her typical "Snake Workplace" one. She smiled and pressed play, practically skipping over to Jagger, who was behind the bar. Hotter Than Hell by Dua Lipa was now playing, and the bar audibly groaned.

"You guys wanted music, so appreciate what you get," Jagger snapped at them, and Sadie blew a kiss to him for her thanks, making him wish he could make another move on her right then. The taste of her on his tongue was burned into his thoughts and he wouldn't stop until he had it straight from the source.

Oh, how he was starting to long for their times in college when it seemed they had all the time in the world to be around each other. Being functioning adults running a business was starting to damper their once carefree friendship. If he was honest, it had been hard to spend much time together since they moved back without work and Travis getting in the way.

Jagger was momentarily distracted by the lyrics and saw Sadie giving him a heated look, which he returned with a grin as he lit up a cigarette from the end of the bar. The sexual tension was high, and he was good at acting cocky when he needed to. He'd grown up surrounded by gang members, and his poker face was as good as anyone else's. He could not, however, pretend that he didn't have a nagging feeling that Sadie was the girl from the app. And now that Travis was out of the way, it made him want to investigate further.

The morning went by quickly, and by the time the lunch crowd was settling, Jagger realized they had been sneaking touches here and there all day. A lingering caress of their fingers when she handed him a beer after popping the top off to push down the bar top, his hand on her waist as he maneuvered behind her to take an order, her hand on his bicep when she needed to ask him to get another case of beer. They were both heated when Jagger excused himself to his office, mumbling about having to check something.

He grabbed the key to the hidden room he kept from inside his desk drawer and tried to think about what he was about to do. Would this be... too much for her? A joke? Destined for a life of friendship and not being able to bend her over this fucking desk after making schedules and sending out paystubs?

Jagger shook off his thoughts and let his dick think for him for a few minutes. He rushed into the room for a moment, coming back with a small black wireless bullet vibrator that had a remote control with 6 different functions on it: Cool, Wow, Amazing, Fuck Me, Holy Shit, and I'm Going To Die.

He slipped it into his back pocket along with the controller, and just as he closed the door behind him and turned the lock, Sadie came rushing in.

"Hey Jag! I need your help with-" she stopped to point at the back door. "What were you doing in the storage? I thought we weren't using it."

"Not a thing," he said, tossing the key back into the drawer and moving towards her.

"Okay, um, anyways," she continued her original thought process with a small smile. "There's a guy that is insisting he gets to drink for free because he knows your dad and said you'd vouch for him."

Jagger nodded and started to usher them out of the office until Sadie put a hand on his chest. "Mind if I take two minutes? I just want to sit down for a second. Everyone else just got topped off, so you won't miss me, promise." She said and moved to sit on the new couch in his office—the one she insisted they needed to take out of their tips last month because the old one's leather was cracking all over the floor.

"I'll still miss you," he drawled as she offered a slow wink. He left her alone and closed the door behind him with a soft click.

Chapter EIGHT

This is my chance, Jagger thought and hurried over to Sadie's phone that was still playing through the speakers. *Lying Is the Most Fun a Girl Can Have Without Taking Off Her Clothes* by Panic! At the Disco now playing and Jagger made a mental note he was going to need to pay more attention to the stuff she played. He brushed past his dad's old friend, Lethal Lenny, with a quick "I'll get you whatever you want! Just give me one second."

Once he had Sadie's phone in his hand, he was careful not to shut the music off. He swiped the playlist off to the side but not before seeing it was called **"Songs I Want To Fuck To."**

Jesus, Sadie, Jagger groaned internally, feeling a twitch in his jeans. No wonder the day had been so taxing on his cock; she had this shit playing in the background all day. He opened the main app screen and scrolled quickly until he saw it.

Jagger's mouth went completely dry and his thumb visibly shook when he clicked on it, opening the app and going right to the 'Messages' section.

And there, in plain sight, were the messages between **RebelsWearLeather** and **BookwormBarbie**.

Fuck, I was right. His mind was racing at this new information. His arousal was pressing hard against his zipper, so he closed out the app, deleted the evidence of his search, and placed the phone back where it was, rushing towards the bar. *La La Lh* by The Dirty Youth now playing as he made his way to Lethal Lenny.

Composing himself behind the bar, he strutted over to the large gentleman. "Haven't seen you in a long time, Len. What can I get for you?" He asked, grabbing a coaster and setting it down before him.

Lethal Lenny grunted, "I know, but some information has come to light that you need to know. Grab me a pitcher. I trust you remember what I like."

With a curt nod, Jagger filled a pitcher of Bud Light and offered him a glass, to which Lethal Lenny waved away. He grabbed the large container and drank right from it, making it look small in his giant hands. Jagger always thought it was funny how the biggest guy in the room wanted the lightest shit in the bar.

"So, tell me." Jagger pressed, referencing his comment earlier.

"Dregs are pulling their shit again. And Jazlyn is with them. They think the Renegades have been keeping their own merchandise in here, fucking up their deals." Lethal

Lenny finished the pitcher and handed it to Jagger for a refill.

"But we don't do that anymore; we haven't done it for a couple of years," Jagger explained, filling the pitcher again. "Sadie and I cleaned this place up and made it safe. Helped the gang to get jobs here and in the community. Real ones."

"Look, I'm just letting you know what I've heard. Do with that information what you will. I know your father still has his hand in some shit, even if he is in fuck-town, Arizona. And I know he's got you on the hook still." Lethal Lenny grabbed his pitcher and stood, towering over everyone around him at the staggering height of 6'8. Jagger always took a moment to appreciate that he was on their side. "I know how hard you've tried to get right, kid. Just trying to help where I can and give you time to move what you gotta if you have to." With that, he returned to the pool table and reunited with some old Rebel buddies.

Jagger leaned back and pinched the bridge of his nose. *Great.*

"You okay, Jaggie?" Sadie asked, appearing by his side and looking flushed.

Jagger straightened and took in her appearance. "Yeah, everything's fine. Are you feeling alright?"

Sadie laughed breathlessly, "Yes, of course. It just got hot in your office. You really gotta put a fan in there."

"I think it's just you, darling." Jagger pulled his lower lip into his mouth, and his teeth dragged along the edges. The sweet little thing fidgeted nervously, her fingers tangling in the bottom of her tresses until he tugged her hands away from her hair. When she froze, his hand reached over and tugged on the hem of her top, pulling it up until the dark lace border of her bra was visible for a beautiful second before letting go. There was a newfound confidence in knowing she wanted him after his discovery, and he decided he would revel in her any chance he could.

Sadie made a pained noise in her throat and grabbed his hand in her own. "Jag, I don't know if you should be touching me. It hasn't been 24 hours since this whole thing with Travis went down, and I haven't even talked to him about it."

Jagger toyed with his bottom lip again as he pulled her closer and leaned down. "I think you're going to come to find I don't need to touch you to get you off, Sweets."

His words ran straight through her, and part of her was curious about what he meant. Before she could ask, he turned her away from the front of the bar and pressed his solid chest against her back. Her hands reached out to brace herself against the shelves that were stocked with liquor along the back wall to keep from her lower half being pushed into the hard edge.

"I promise I won't touch you. For now."

The promise in his voice had wetness pooling between her thighs in an instant.

"I'll tell you what. I can walk away right now and stop playing this game you started when you began letting Camille cut up these tiny ass tops," The toe of his boot kicked against hers. "And bought these fucking boots," His hands fisted in the sides of his old jacket she was wearing despite how hot she claimed to be a moment ago. "And started wearing one of my old Rebel skins like a damn varsity jacket." His voice dropped low as he pressed his mouth to her ear, lips tickling the shell. "Or you can pretend to clean one of these bottles, and I'll take that as a sign that you want me to keep going."

Sadie was practically hyperventilating, panting as if she'd run a mile as her grip tightened on the cool counter of the ledge. She knew she already lost the game the second he turned her around, and she felt how hard he was against her ass, their jeans doing nothing to hide it. She reached behind her to run her hand down the side of his face, which was still in the crook of her neck, before reaching for a bottle of Tito's and a rag in front of her.

Jagger growled his approval in her ear, "Good girl." He shifted to the side to shield their actions from the nearly empty bar, thanking his lucky stars that most had cleared out already. Regardless of how tired he was from his late-night exertions hiding both drugs and, yes, a body or two, he was thrumming with energy. Quickly, he plucked the small vibrator from his pocket and snaked his hand to the front of her pelvis. His fingers brushing against the base skin of her stomach sent a shiver through her, the cold metal of his rings biting her flesh. Suddenly he was sliding his hand with the bullet inside the front of her jeans as Sadie sucked in her breath, allowing him more space to fit against the denim.

"Good *fucking* girl," Jagger said again, and in one more motion, the bullet was nestled between her folds on top of her clit. It almost killed him to leave the silken heat that beckoned him, but he took a deep breath and slipped his hand out. Kissing her cheek, he stepped away and held his arms up innocently.

Sadie looked at him over the bottle she was holding, and her eyes showed that she was simultaneously turned on and confused.

Jagger smirked and said, "I won't touch you, but I can't promise you won't cum in front of these strangers right here."

When Sadie gently touched the front of her jeans, and looked down to see what he'd done, his dark chuckle snapped her focus back to him. Reveling in the moment, he opened his palm to show that he had a small black remote in his hand.

Sadie's eyes widened as the realization of what he'd put down her pants became obvious.

Jagger made a dramatic motion of his finger coming down to press the 'ON' button, and she yelped against the vibrations on her clit, dropping the bottle of liquor with a **_CRASH_** and earning several looks from the remaining few in the bar. *Cool.* Jagger smiled and pressed the remote again, kicking it up another notch.

"I'll watch the bar while you clean that up," he said and handed her a rag. "And you... you better put on your game face when you come back. I can assure you it's definitely giving us away right now."

Sadie blushed and watched as he sauntered back to tend the bar, slipping the remote in his front pocket. She crouched down, causing the vibrator to press hard against her clit with the positioning against the seam of her jeans. *Wow.* Sadie braced herself against a cooler and quickly cleaned up the mess, putting the glass pieces and dirty rag in a small trash bin. She was surprised she didn't cut herself because of how shaky she was.

"Sadie?!"

Sadie looked up from her spot on the ground, securely hidden from the bar's front entrance. Jagger gave her a sideways glance from where he was standing before her, as he popped open a few beers and handed them off to a couple of older gentlemen. There were a few seconds spent before pushing his long sleeves up his forearms, exposing a few of Sadie's favorite tattoos that he had. A quote from Aristotle, *"We are what we repeatedly do,"* woven with barbed wire and the bleeding roses that he constantly added to his left arm - he never explained why, but every so often, he would add another rose or two over the years. There had to be at least two dozen now, but he would just wink at her and say he 'always wanted to have a garden, but didn't have the time.'

Sadie gulped.

"Where's Sadie?"

It was Travis.

Of course.

Of course, he'd be here right now.

The universe hated her, she was sure.

Jagger angled his body directly in front of her, shielding her from Travis's inquiring eyes.

"Hey, Travis. Wasn't expecting you tonight." Jagger's tone was brisk.

Travis grabbed a seat at one of the stools and leaned in, elbows resting on the bartop as his hands massaged his temples. "Where is she, Wilder? She's supposed to be working today and won't answer my calls."

Jagger shrugged. "Not sure I'm comfortable telling you after what happened this morning."

"She doesn't know what she heard," Travis said, clearly miffed that Jagger knew what had transpired between them before he had a chance to fix it. "It wasn't what it sounded like."

Raising a disbelieving eyebrow, Jagger leaned his hip against one of the coolers nestled under the bar top, unconsciously hitting the remote against it and turning the vibrations to another level.

Amazing.

There was another shift in his hips.

Fuck me.

Sadie's hand flew to her mouth to keep a scream from coming out as her other hand grasped Jagger's calf with the other. Jagger grunted in surprise and let out a loud cough. He then slammed a hand on the bar top to distract Travis from his outburst. "Look, Trav. I know exactly what we heard."

"We? Why were you with her?"

Desperate to get hold of a public orgasm at work, little Miss Sweetwater bit her lip and tried desperately to undo her jeans and take the damn thing out.

"Why weren't you?" Jagger bit back before answering his question sarcastically. "Oh yeah, you were busy fucking someone. And let's be honest here, Trav. It's not the first time you've done it, is it?"

Travis launched over the bar top, grabbing Jagger by the collar of his shirt and pulling him onto the hard surface. "You better watch your mouth, Wilder!"

The remote was pressed again, sending Sadie's body into overdrive, and a scream tore through her throat. *Holy Shit.*

Both of the men paused, not being able to deny the fact that Sadie was under the bar.

"Sadie?" Travis called over the bar, releasing his hold on Jagger. He watched as she stood behind the Serpent Pit owner, eyeing her unbuttoned jeans.

"The fuck -"

Sadie interrupted him, the vibrator raging inside her soaked folds, leaving her voice thick. "Travis, we don't need to talk about anything," she gritted out. "I'm not even mad. We weren't working. I knew this, and now you knew we weren't, too." She paused to catch her breath. "But you need to leave."

Sadie grabbed onto the counter, her body doubling over from the intense pleasure and almost painful sensation of trying not to cum in front of patrons and her boyfriend. Screw that, ex-boyfriend.

"I'm serious."

Impressed didn't even come close to how Jagger felt with how well she was handling the situation. That is, considering he never got to turn the bullet off. Travis was scrutinizing him so hard the moment the asshole walked through the door that he knew it was unwise to draw attention to anything. And that included reaching down to take the remote out of his pocket to turn it off, so he prayed she'd be able to keep herself in check.

He put his hand on her lower back in a supportive gesture, and his eyebrows shot up as he felt the vibrations under his hand.

Oh, fuck. That's not right, Jagger thought as his usual collected demeanor changed, and he started; *how high is this fucking thing turned up?*

Sadie's head bowed, and her hair fell over her reddened face like a dark curtain of sunshine. Travis put his hands over hers, and she let out a primal growl, "Don't touch me."

Jagger needed to save her.

"You heard her." Lethal Lenny, the giant with the raging gray beard, and the other two playing pool had come over from all the commotion. "My friends will walk you out."

"Fine." He relented and started to turn away. "You were bringing me down anyway. Working at this shitty bar. Christ, you weren't even good in bed."

"Funny. That's what she said about you," Jagger interrupted. Travis tried to grab for him again, but Lethal Lenny grabbed him by his high school coaching sweater, and they began leading him out of the building.

"Have a good night, boss!" The youngest of the trio, Scales, yelled over his shoulder. "We got this."

The remaining few customers followed behind, and once everyone was out the door, Sadie turned into Jagger, clutching her arms around his neck and moaning into his chest.

"Fuck, Sweets. I didn't mean to." Jagger scrambled to get the remote from his pocket with one hand while the other held her around the waist, keeping her upright. "I'm turning it off, baby." He reassured her.

Sadie pulled back and gripped his raven hair, catching his gaze. "Don't you fucking dare."

Jagger dropped the remote with a final 'click' on the ground before lifting Sadie onto the back counter. Her back slammed into the shelves lined with bottles as she wrapped her legs around his waist.

"Kiss me." She begged, fingers digging into his scalp as she tried to pull his face to hers. The storm inside was rising up through her body, unable to withstand any more assault on her hot center, and her clit was screaming against the onslaught of prolonged stimulation. Jagger's mouth crashed down upon hers as her back arched into him, not unlike in the freezer the night before.

But this time, she was coming undone in his arms.

I'm going to die.

Their kiss was frenzied, eager, and filled with such pent-up emotion it sent Sadie entirely over the edge. She screamed his name inside his open mouth while he gripped her hips so hard he was sure she'd wear the mark of his fingertips for weeks. As Sadie's orgasm rippled through her, Jagger brought her back onto the floor so he could still hold her. Watching as she panted, he grabbed the remote off the floor, turning it off and relieving Sadie.

"Christ, Jag," Sadie whispered, pushing herself away from him as she collected herself. She finished unzipping her jeans and fished the bullet from her wet depths.

"I think this belongs to you," she said, handing it over to Jagger, who was warring with himself on whether or not to take her on top of the goddamn bar. But she said no touching. And they were already pushing that limit with their kiss.

And holy hell, what a kiss.

Jagger took a shuddering breath. "Thank you," He murmured and ran his open mouth along the black silicone toy, her juices catching the neon lights flickering around them. A low growl escaped his throat, and his eyes closed as he savored her taste.

Stunned silence filled the bar as she watched him, suddenly feeling self-conscious as he cleaned the vibrator thoroughly with slow laps of his tongue. "It's closing time, so uh..." She shifted on her feet, feeling slightly uncomfortable from the wetness in her jeans.

Jagger looked expectantly at her. "You want me to close up while you clean up?" He offered, placing the toy in his pocket.

Sadie nodded.

Jagger nodded back, "Of course."

Sadie started making her way to the bathrooms, stumbling on what felt like sea legs from the forceful orgasm she just had in her friend's arms. She could hear Jagger collecting the empty beer bottles from around the bar.

"Um, Jag?" She stalled. "Do you want to watch a movie or something tonight?"

Jagger paused his task and looked over at her. She wasn't facing him, but her hands fisted at her sides.

"Like old times?" He asked, his voice sounding hope-ful.

God, she loved him like this.

"Like old times," Sadie agreed and started walking again, but you could hear the smile in her voice when she spoke next.

"And then afterward, maybe we can talk about the sex dungeon you have hidden in the storage room."

Chapter
NINE

Sadie held her breath as she waited for Jagger to unlock the door to his apartment upstairs. The way he was fumbling with his keys tipped her off that she wasn't the only one who was a bundle of nerves.

When Jagger managed to swing the door open and gesture for Sadie to move into the space, she tossed her jacket onto the chair beside the bed before taking a seat. As her weight fell onto the bed, the mattress groaned, the springs giving a small resistance to the girl on top of it.

Jagger locked the door behind them before turning to face Sadie, who was casually lounging on the edge of his bed, looking like a picture of perfect sin - still dressed in all black, a flush still on her cheeks from her orgasm downstairs in the bar. He hadn't meant it to go quite like that, but he was definitely not complaining about how it ended.

Sadie certainly was not, either.

Jagger plopped down into the chair beside the bed, putting his jacket with hers. As he reached down to remove his boots, he muttered, "As much as I love you in those clothes, I'm not going to be able to focus on a movie if you're next to me like that."

Sadie leaned back and balanced on her elbows, trying to look inviting.

"Should I take them off then?" The tantalizing way her words shook him made him look up from his task.

Jagger cursed as he threw the boots against the wall and charged to his dresser.

"Like that's much better," he whined, almost pitifully. Settling on a white T-shirt and red plaid pajamas that should work for Sadie and grabbing the gray sweatpants he was wearing the other day for himself, he presented her with the clothing. "Here."

Sadie pouted and sat up to grab them from his outstretched hand. She wouldn't admit it, but she was excited to get into something comfortable after the long day they had, even if it was barely 7:00 p.m. now. She started to lift her shirt over her head, and Jagger spun around to give her some privacy. It was a surprising and kind gesture, considering that he had literally shoved a vibrator down her jeans while she was working tonight.

Jagger knew better than to watch her get undressed, not trusting himself to keep his hands off of her. He could hear her shifting on the bed and the rustle of fabric, her shirt hitting the ground, and the pull of her zipper. He swallowed and quickly shed his own clothes before pulling on his sweatpants.

Clearing his throat but needing to break the tension, he asked, "So, what do you want to watch?"

"Anything is fine, I'm just excited to lay down," Sadie said honestly, the promise of relaxation looming.

Jagger turned around, confident he had given her enough time to change and crawled onto the bed to join her after grabbing the remote. She still looked far too good, even in his baggy shirt, the rest of her body under his covers. Jagger wrapped an arm around her as she snuggled up and settled beside him, her arm across his bare stomach. They had done this a dozen times, and even though they had shared some intimate moments the past week, nothing felt more comforting than being close to her best friend.

They were silent as Jagger clicked through some Netflix suggestions before putting on Django Unchained, Sadie's favorite Tarantino film. He felt her smile against his chest as it started playing, and her breath tickled him as she asked, "Are you ready to talk about your 'red room of pain', Mr. Gray?" Sadie teased.

Jagger's arm tightened around her shoulders, and his head fell against his modest wooden headboard. "Can't we just enjoy the movie?" he pleaded.

Sadie giggled, and it had a dangerous quality that made Jagger nervous.

"Oh, please. We've both seen this movie a dozen times. However, I have never seen a playroom before, and I am *dying* to know what my best friend has been doing there."

"I don't know," he admitted honestly. "It was just something that interested me. I guess I spent my life obeying orders and wanted to see what it was like on the other side. The feeling of control and having someone submit to you completely is exhilarating."

"Have you done a lot?" She asked gently, trying not to be too jealous at the thought of Jagger and this other side of him she didn't know until tonight.

"I've had a few submissives," he answered carefully. "Nothing long-term, and more for the learning process and knowledge that needed to be addressed. They were fully aware that I was starting out and offered to help."

"So, like, they let you practice on them?" She asked, looking to understand.

Jagger sighed. "Yeah."

A hand threaded through his hair as he willed himself to calm down, the topic of choice with the person he'd wanted to build that room for in his arms asking about it making him nervous. "In a sense, we kind of helped each other. They were new to being a sub as well. We experimented and tested boundaries and researched."

"It sounds more like work than sex." Sadie wrinkled her nose.

Jagger laughed, and Sadie raised her head and shifted to look up at him. "In the beginning, it is," he admitted. "If you want to learn how to be safe about it. It's not like you can jump into this stuff blindly; you need to put in the work to get good at it. Like anything in life."

"Are you," Sadie paused to bite her lower lip. "Are you good at it now?"

Jagger dared to look down at Sadie, who was looking at him with lust and curiosity, and his Adam's apple
bobbed as he found his voice. "I think I'm pretty decent."

With a nod, she acknowledged that information and
snuggled back into her place on his chest. "Will you
teach me?" She asked after a pause, her voice so quiet
he wasn't sure what he heard her say at first.

Jagger exhaled with a hiss. "It's not so much about
teaching when it comes to submission. It's about trust.
You'd have to trust me, Sweets. You'd have to completely trust me with your body and mind."

Sadie let out a little yawn, her eyelids heavy. The
peace of being in Jagger's arms was causing her to feel
heavy with exhaustion.

"But I already do trust you," she whispered, and her
fingers traced the snake on his hip.

"I know, baby." Jagger kissed her forehead, brushing
her hair out of her face with a gentle swipe of his
fingers. "You better after that time I saved your ass when
we went hiking."

Sadie's laughter shook her shoulders as she tried
to defend herself. "I did not need saving! I merely
slipped!" She kicked his leg lightly as she pulled herself
closer to him.

Jagger rolled his eyes, and then his strong fingers
were on her side, tickling her until she was peeling with
laughter.

"Stop!" Sadie pleaded with tears streaming down
her face from the onslaught of his attack. "Jag!"

Jagger's smile was warm when he let up and pulled her back onto his chest, her laughter quieting.

"I hate hiking," he admitted, seemingly out of nowhere.

Sadie sounded confused when she spoke. "But you always went hiking with me during college."

Jagger shrugged, slumping down the headboard so he was almost lying down with Sadie on the bed. "You liked it, and I didn't want you going on those trails by yourself. I know what's out there and how easily men want to eat you up. Besides, it gave me an excuse to touch you often when you lost your balance every ten minutes."

"Doesn't seem like you need much of an excuse lately." Sadie teased.

"You're right."

"I know."

"Good."

"Well, I feel like today has certainly been enlightening."

You have no idea, Jagger's mind whispered, thinking back to finding that stupid app on her phone.

"About my lifestyle and that room-" Jagger took a deep breath. "It's not something I expected you to know about until much later. I'm sure some of the stuff there might have surprised you."

"Not really," she admitted. "I was more turned on imagining myself in there. Tied up to the wall with those restraints you had hanging -"

Jagger covered her mouth gently with a deep groan ripping from his throat. "You're going to kill me." He removed his hand and rested it on her bicep before kissing her head again.

"We can talk about it more another time. You're exhausted, and my self-control is lacking when you're around on the best of days, let alone after making you cum in those tight jeans."

Sadie let out a tired laugh and smiled. "Fine. Mind if I crash here tonight? I'll have to leave early to get to The Upside Scoop tomorrow and meet my mom anyway."

"I wasn't letting you go home. It's been too long since we've had time together like this, and I'm going to be greedy."

Sadie couldn't see his grin but heard it in his voice.

"I like it when you're greedy," she sighed and was out moments later.

Jagger watched as Sadie fell asleep on his chest and played with her thick golden hair, gently combing his fingers through it. He wanted to tell her he knew it was her from the app, but with her new knowledge of his playroom, he decided against it. They would be apart for the next few days while she worked with her mom during the week, and it would give him time to figure out their changing dynamic.

The sound of gunshots from the screen startled him, and he clicked the television off to succumb to the pull of sleep with his Sadie wrapped around him.

Chapter TEN

"You look like a mess, Sadira!" Karen Sweetwater screeched as she took in Sadie's appearance. Storming over to Sadie while she typed away at her laptop on the small desk in the corner, she raised an accusatory finger in her face.

"Did you even shower? Is that leftover makeup?" She immediately reached out to smooth the flyaways from Sadie's normally perfect ponytail.

Sadie batted her hand away, eyes still fixed on her computer screen. "I woke up late and only had time to freshen up and throw on new clothes," she explained and continued to type.

Karen was not placated. "I can't believe you're still working at that nasty bar. Isn't it time you grew up and focused on your career?"

Sadie paused while typing to glare at her mother.

"I can assure you that my career will still be there after the bar gets back on its feet." She turned her attention back to the computer before continuing, "Or you just acknowledge that I do most of the work here, too."

Karen gasped, "Sadira Sweetwater! That is no way to speak to me. Is this because of Travis?"

Sadie took a deep breath and resisted punching the computer screen. *When did I get so violent?*

"Travis is an amazing man, Sadira. You were lucky to be with him. He could have given you anything you wanted-"

Except for orgasms, Sadie's thoughts overlapped her mother's rantings. *Or communication. Or chemistry.*

"And furthermore, you need to start being more responsible."

"Duly noted, mom," Sadie grinds out. "But Travis and I haven't been working for a long time. And he's been seeing someone else, so I thought the *responsible* thing to do in that situation was to break up."

Karen opened her mouth to say something, but Sadie cut her off.

"Now, if you could let me focus, I want to have this article edited and ready for publication tomorrow."

With a huff, Karen turned and walked back to her desk.

The day dragged on, and Sadie wanted to text Jagger and tell him what a bitch her mom was being, but she knew he was alone at the bar on Mondays, and he was probably busy.

I can call him later, Sadie thought but still pouted about it.

Eventually, she glanced at her mother, who was conducting a phone interview in the other room, and slid her phone out from her purse.

Sadie opened up her SecretScape app and typed up a new post:

'After today, I think I need a good fuck.'

She quickly hid her phone under the desk as her mom breezed through the room to grab a folder from one of the filing cabinets. She felt a rush of excitement course through her when she felt the familiar buzzing that indicated that she had a new notification and peeked at her screen.

RebelsWearLeather:

> I wish I could help with that.

Sadie bit her lip and responded quickly as Karen returned to the other room.

BookwormBarbie:

> You might be able to help with something else.

RebelsWearLeather:

> Sexting again? ;)

Sadie laughed out loud and then cleared her throat to cover it when her mother shot her a dark look.

BookwormBarbie:

> That was great, but I'm in the middle of something right now. And hopefully, seeing someone. I was actually going to ask if you could answer some questions about BDSM.

RebelsWearLeather:

> Seeing someone, huh? That was fast. Is it who you've been pining for?

Sadie hastily typed a response, understanding how quick it seemed to the stranger, and wanted to backtrack. Because, well, they weren't seeing each other, were they?

BookwormBarbie:

> Yeah. Well, I guess I jumped the gun. We're not seeing each other ... yet, but I want to.

RebelsWearLeather:

> So, what's the problem?

BookwormBarbie:

He's in this whole lifestyle, and I'm worried I will mess up being his submissive.

There was a long pause. Sadie started to fidget nervously and pluck at a piece of tape stuck on her desk. The task caused her to barely notice Karen slipping out of the office, and as she glanced at the clock, she realized it was almost time to go home. Karen was probably running one last errand. Whatever the case, Sadie sat back in her chair to give her attention fully to her conversation with her internet James Dean to better understand her real-life leather-wearing bad boy.

RebelsWearLeather:

Gotcha. Hence the question about BDSM.

RebelsWearLeather:

Well, what would you like to know? I'm here to help in any way that I can.

BookwormBarbie:

How do I know what to do?

RebelsWearLeather:

He will tell you.

BookwormBarbie:

But what if I don't want to do it, or I don't listen?

RebelsWearLeather:

> Then you don't have to do it. Unless you refuse to do something just to rile him up. Then you'll be punished. Or rewarded.

RebelsWearLeather:

> Depends on how you look at it.

RebelsWearLeather:

> And you need to figure out your safe word.

BookwormBarbie:

> Okay...

There was another pause, and Sadie set her phone down and began to get her things together, stuffing papers in her bag and dreaming of a nice warm shower at home. It seemed like their conversation was over until her screen lit up again.

RebelsWearLeather:

> How about this - why don't you tell me what you want him to do. Clearly, you're okay with some more intense acts. And per our other conversation, being tied up isn't out of the question either.

A flush swept across Sadie's cheek as she remembered how brazen she'd been all weekend.

BookwormBarbie:

> Yeah, I'd like those. I've always had a fantasy of being tied up and eaten out while blindfolded.

RebelsWearLeather:

> That's a great place to start.

BookwormBarbie:

And maybe nipple clamps.

RebelsWearLeather:

Now we're talking.

Sadie bit her lip and cursed out loud. She shouldn't be getting this turned on talking about this... should she? Grabbing her jacket and closing up the office behind her, she made her way to her car. Settling inside and turning it on, she sent another message.

BookwormBarbie:

Is this conversation weird?

BookwormBarbie:

Am I weird?

RebelsWearLeather:

Haha, no. If you can't ask a stranger online, who can you ask right?

RebelsWearLeather:

But you should talk to him about all this. I'm sure he would love to explore all of this with you.

RebelsWearLeather:

I'd relax and see what happens.

BookwormBarbie:

Thanks for your help! Sorry, this wasn't as exciting as last time ;)

RebelsWearLeather:

> On the contrary. By the way, I heard a song you
> might like. I'll send you a link to it.

RebelsWearLeather:

> *Liar in a Red Dress / Adam Jensen / Listen Here*

Sadie clicked the link and let the music flow through
her stereo. It had an excellent beat, but she was more
excited that such a sexy song made someone think of her.

BookwormBarbie:

> I like it. A lot. I'll have to add it to my playlist :)

RebelsWearLeather:

> You do that, darling.

Jagger planned to avoid being caught off guard by Jazlyn
Evler on what was supposed to be a slow Monday night at
the Pit.

He had just finished stocking the bar and was enjoying a smoke while watching some Rebels and North

Siders enjoy each other's company over drinks, pool, and conversation. The dancer scheduled that evening hadn't shown up, but no one seemed to mind, so Jagger didn't try to get anyone else in to cover her shift.

He looked forward to a calm night where he could think about his little discussion with BookwormBarbie.

But fucking Jazlyn was in his face.

"I know it's here, Wilder," she growled. "Tell me where the merchandise is. You know the drill; this is my territory."

Jagger took a drag from his cigarette and purposefully blew the smoke in Jazlyn's face from across the bar top.

"The Rebels, especially me, don't run drugs anymore."

Jazlyn signaled behind her, and over a dozen Dregs started pouring in from the entrance.

"I don't believe you. Someone has been cutting into our clientele, and I know the reason is because you're selling some shit. I'm gonna find it and cut 'em off, so the town will have to come back to us for their fix." Jazlyn said, waving the smoke away.

Jagger shrugged his shoulders, the cigarette hanging from his lips as he braced both hands on the bar to lean closer to Jazlyn. "You're welcome to look around." He gestured to the floor of the room where the Dregs were already scouring, trying to question the customers and look for places he may have hidden his 'stock.' "But you might as well grab a drink. You'll be here a long time trying to find something that doesn't exist."

Jazlyn rolled her eyes.

"So what can I get you?"

Sadie had just finished drying her hair, thankful to finally have a shower to clean up after the last 24 hours. She threw on some black lingerie and checked herself out in the floor-length mirror at the corner of her room, wondering if this would be something Jagger would like to see her in someday. She had bought it on a whim and never bothered to wear it for Travis. He didn't really care about anything sexy like this. He was more into her white lace frilly outfits than her darker aesthetic.

She slipped a short red dress over the lingerie tucked away in her closet, waiting for a chance to come out and play, and smiled.

She looked good. *Great*, actually.

Sadie smoothed down the dress and continued to fantasize about Jagger seeing her like this, properly dressed up and enticing him with her curves. A far cry from the book smart girl he met and more like the woman she was blossoming into.

The ringing of her phone brought her back to reality from her thoughts and she snatched it from her purse, excited to see it was Jagger. She had called him when she got home but figured since she got his voicemail that he was still busy.

"Hi!" She chirped, a smile on her face already.

"Sadie!" Jagger shouted through the earpiece, and Sadie had to pull the phone away from her head, wincing at the loud music coursing through it. "I need a favor!"

Sadie sat on her bed, the dress riding up her thighs, and her smile faltered.

"Are you alright?"

"Yeah! Look, I don't have time to explain. Can you call the dancers to see if they can come in?"

She could hear static that sounded like Jagger was trying to cover the phone with his hand while he yelled at someone in the bar. "Scales! You alright? Get over here!"

"Are you sure everything is okay? It sounds crazy over there! I can come in-"

Jagger cut her off. "*No*! I do *not* want you to come here. Do you understand? Just see if the girls can come in." There was a loud crash in the background. "You were right. They help distract these guys, and I need someone on the stage."

Sadie started to argue again, but Jagger insisted. "I'm serious; stay *home*."

Click.

There was no way Sadie was listening to that when it sounded like the bar was being torn apart. She didn't bother changing and instead threw on her motorcycle boots, grabbed her purse, and flew out the door.

Sadie walked in through the back door of the Serpent Pit, deciding that trying the front entrance would be pointless from seeing all the gang members arguing in front of the doors. She had called the few girls they had hired to dance at the bar on her frantic drive over, but none of them could come in and cover tonight.

She barely registered what she was doing until she climbed the steps onto the dark stage. The sight before her a mess; Jagger and Scales desperately trying to separate Dregs and Renegades in the midst of flying limbs. As her eyes scanned the crowd she noticed a blonde woman in the middle of the bar, looking pleased with herself and narrowed her eyes.

This must be that bitch I've heard about. Sadie's mind growled, thinking back to when Jagger explained the rival gang of the Dregs and how much he had struggled to cut ties with their leader.

Jazlyn, wasn't it?

Sadie crouched next to the stereo system and grabbed the phone plugged into the speakers; Dreg gang signs were carved into the case. She tossed it to the ground and heard a satisfying crack while she hastily plugged her own phone in and hit play on the most recent song—the one RebelWearsLeather sent her.

Switching on the stage lights, she didn't even bother to take off her boots as she walked over to the pole.

It took a few moments before *I'm a Sucker for a Liar in a Red Dress* by Adam Jensen started blaring, but when it did, she took note of the yelling in the bar as it started to lessen. Eyes were beginning to drift over to her as she moved around the solid steel bar that had become a part of her these last few months.

Her eyes connected with Jagger's as she dipped around the pole and lifted her leg to assist in arching backward, awarding her onlookers with a sensual toss of her hair. She was pleased with the fact that his jaw was practically on the floor, and she made a subtle gesture of her head to get him back on task, signaling, *'Get them out of here!'.*

Sadie grinned to herself as he tore his gaze away, but not after his eyes undressed her once or twice. She turned her back to him and her audience and began circling her hips in a figure-8 motion. When she faced the crowd again, she could see Jagger and Scales move around the bar of now distracted customers and start to clear out the Dregs one by one.

Sadie could feel everyone's eyes on her, thrilled her more than she'd ever admit. But still, nothing compared to the glances that Jagger was throwing at her as he moved around the floor while she spun around the pole. His eyes were darker than she'd ever seen before, and wetness already began gathering between her legs as she began to strip off her red dress, bringing it up over her head and tossing it to the side.

When the music swelled again, Sadie slid her back down the pole, the cold steel rubbing against her spine as she descended onto her knees in the middle of the stage. She crawled to the edge and pulled a cigarette from one of the Dreg member's mouth, dangling it between her slim fingers as she swung her legs over the side of the stage and wrapped them around his shoulders, her black panties barely keeping anything to the imagination this close to eye-level. She barely noticed the hoots and hollers of the crowd around her, encouraging her forward.

Fuck it.

She sucked deep from the cigarette and blew the smoke directly in the face of the shocked gangbanger before twisting, her thighs catching him around the neck and banging his head off the lip of the stage. The now unconscious Dreg slowly slipped from her legs and slumped to the ground.

Sadie dropped the cigarette onto the back of his jacket and stood on his back, using the stage as leverage as she braced herself for the descent. She looked into Jazlyn's eyes, who was staring at her, and stubbed the lit cigarette into the stitched Dreg emblem of a rat on a motorcycle on the jacket with her boot, looking sinister and sexy at the same time.

Sadie watched Jagger moving back from the entrance, trying to get through the now smaller crowd to get to her, looking every bit like he was going to either stop this whole show or fuck her in front of everyone.

Sadie smiled, filled with excitement. And she wasn't even done yet.

Jazlyn visibly gulped as Sadie walked straight towards her, running her hands over her chest and teasing her nipples through her see-through lace bralette.

Sadie vaguely heard the Dreg's body being picked off the ground and moved out of the building as she stood in front of Jazlyn, bringing her hand up to wrap around the back of her neck. Jazlyn's eyes were hooded, and she was drinking in the vision of the blonde goddess before her, completely hypnotized.

Sadie licked her bottom lip, and when Jazlyn's eyes landed on her moist mouth, she tightened her grip on her neck and crashed her lips against the Dreg leader's. Their tongues danced together, and Jazlyn's arms wrapped around Sadie's waist, clinging to her in a moment of reck-lessness.

"Holy, sweet shit!" Sadie heard Scales gasp from some-where in the bar.

The grin spread along her face before she pulled back from Jazlyn, eyes locking onto hers as the other blonde woman panted, clearly disoriented.

The song had ended, and the bar was dead silent.

"Get. *Out.*" Sadie whispered against her lips and re-leased her hold on her neck, laughing as Jazlyn stumbled backward right into Jagger's arms as he stood behind her.

He growled something in her ear, all the while staring at Sadie, and in an instant, she was scrambling for the door, the rest of the Dregs following after her.

Jagger didn't take his eyes off her, even when the roars of the Serpents erupted around them in triumph over getting the Dregs out of their safe haven. They stood looking at each other for what felt like an eternity until Jagger lifted his hand to quiet everyone down and spoke.

"Bar's closed!" He shouted. "Everyone out. Now."

The tone of his voice left no room to question him.

Sadie's eyes darted nervously as the rest of the customers approached them and outside. She offered a shaky smile to Scales, who mouthed 'good luck' to her on his way out.

And then, they were utterly alone in the bar.

"Jag," Sadie started, putting her hands up in a 'calm down' gesture. "I was just trying to-"

Jagger moved toward her and hoisted her over his shoulder, his arm snug around her waist while he gave a sharp spank to her backside with the other.

"What are you doing?!" She hissed from the pain but melted against him from the pleasure rippling through her that followed.

"Clearly something I should have done a long time ago," he hissed as he stormed his way into the office. He set her down for a moment to grab the keys from his desk that unlocked the back room. Jagger was still holding onto her waist when he unlocked the door and guided her into the dimly lit room filled with... playthings.

Jagger watched her face as panic and lust dueled inside Sadie as she was brought over to what looked like a giant X with cuffs bolted to it against the wall.

"Jag..." She pleaded, her eyes wide.

He grabbed both of her hands and stretched them above her head, taking turns securing her wrists in the leather cuffs.

"Do you have any idea what you did to me?" His tone was so deep that it sounded like the crash of waves from the ocean, and he bit his lip as he watched her shiver.

Jagger grabbed her throat with his left hand, and his open mouth was torturing the spot behind her right ear when he continued. "Do you know how fucking hard I was the second I saw you up there?" He licked her pulse point and dragged his mouth down her collarbone, delighting in her little moans of pleasure.

"What did you think would happen?" There was a yelp when he bit into the flesh above the swell of her breast. "Tell me. What did you think would happen when you decided to go on that goddamn stage and dance to that song?" He groaned and sucked a nipple into his mouth through the lace of her bra.

Sadie's head slammed back against the wall as she cried out, and Jagger's hand around her neck slid behind it to force her forward, making her stare down into his eyes as he looked up from where he was now teasing her breast with his teeth.

Sadie shuddered, her voice sounding small in the room when she spoke. "I was just trying to help."

"Oh, you helped. I'll give you that. But you completely fucked me up, Sweets." Jagger growled and sank to his knees before her, his dark hair falling before his eyes. He grabbed her leather-wrapped ankle before holding it higher to access the back of her knee and gave the flesh a slow lick with the length of his tongue.

"I'm sorry!" She squeaked out in surprise as his teeth sank into her calf before kissing the abused flesh.

"So am I. This is not how I imagined bringing you in here the first time." His admission sounded strained against her knee as he spread her legs apart slightly so they'd reach the ankle cuffs dangling towards the ground beside them. "But you looked like *goddamn* sex on that stage." He licked the side of her boot until his tongue met the skin of her shin above it. "And you wore these fucking boots!" He snarled and hastily took the boots off before throwing them behind him, the heavy sounds bouncing off the walls around them.

"You know what those things do to me, baby." He groaned and fastened her ankles into the remaining cuffs.

The sounds of Sadie trying to hold back her moan still came out as a whimper. And it was driving him insane.

"I know." She whispered and desperately tried to close her legs, seeming embarrassed by the feeling of her arousal seeping through her panties so close to his face.

Jagger couldn't figure out why. He wanted to bury his face between her legs and drown in her.

Trying to calm himself, he grabbed onto both her thighs with his large hands, his rings cold against her skin as he rested his forehead against her pelvis, his breath tickling her pussy through the lace. "I know you wanted a blindfold, but I want you to look at me the first time I make you cum with my mouth." He said quietly.

He could feel her eyes on him as he shrugged his shoulders. "And the nipple clamps will have to wait, too. I don't even trust myself to take your fucking clothes off right now."

Sadie's sharp intake of breath at his words caused him to steel himself and rise onto his feet to stand before her. He brushed a lone strand of hair that had fallen in front of her face back behind her ear and cupped her face tenderly with his warm palm.

"I must be crazy," she sputtered, shaking her head. "You're not..." Her voice trailed off as he approached.

A nervous laugh drifted out of Jagger as he leaned forward to kiss her mouth, bracing his hands against the wall on either side of her head.

"Did you have enough time to pick that safe word yet?" He let his words caress her lips before he pulled back to look at her again.

"Rebel? You're that Rebel?" Sadie choked out, her eyes searching his face frantically for the answer she was seeking.

Jagger gave her one of his lopsided grins.

"Yeah, Barbie. It's me."

Sadie swore her soul must have left her body before it came crashing back, racking her body with a shudder that rattled the chains of her vices.

Oh, my god, her mind churned. *I masturbated with him and had that conversation today. I -*

"Sadie," Jagger said firmly, grasping her chin to stare deep into her eyes. "Stop spiraling."

Sadie exhaled loudly, willing herself to collect her nerves. "How long?"

How long have you known? Her mind was screaming.

Jagger gave her a brilliant smile, and she could have sworn she saw a blush cross his cheeks. How in the world he had any right to be embarrassed when she was throwing herself at him online and in person was beyond her.

"I had suspicions the other day but wasn't sure until yesterday."

Sadie blinked a few times, staring at the boy she had turned her whole world upside down for once already. His friendship had meant everything to her, and she loved being in this town again, if it meant being with her best friend, helping him keep his family business open. Supporting each other.

And apparently, wanting to fuck each other's brains out now.

"So that conversation today..." She trailed off, dropping her gaze to stare at the ground, taking in her cuffed ankles while Jagger laughed.

"Yeah, darling. That was me. And I meant it when I said I'd love to explore this with you." Her eyes shot back up to his, and his smile had her returning it with her own.

"I'd love to do this like we've done everything since we met." He pressed a soft kiss to her mouth. "Together."

"I trust you," Sadie whispered against his mouth.

It was all the encouragement he needed to continue.

Jagger started kissing his way down her body. Hot breath tickled her chest as his mouth moved between her breasts and across her ribcage. His tongue dipped inside her navel before trailing over to her hip and biting the skin softly, drawing a high-pitched squeak from her parted mouth. Part of her knew where this was going; she had craved it all week. But now that he was kneeling between her thighs and she was strapped to this thing, she felt her nerves pile up again.

What the fuck is this thing, honestly? She mused before crying out when she felt Jagger's calloused finger slide through the side of her panties to tease her entrance. "Jag," she whined and tried hopelessly to bring his finger inside her, wanting - no, *needing* him to fill her.

"That's it, baby," he whispered against the lace on her crotch, his hot breath warming her center even more, which she thought was impossible because she was already in flames. "Beg for me. I want you to beg for my fingers, and my tongue, and my-"

"Christ, Jag!" Sadie yelled, incredulous. "What the fuck do you think I'm doing?"

Jagger's chuckle was dark, like the look in his eyes, when his gaze roamed up her body and caught hers.

"You're not begging yet, Sweets." He pushed his finger all the way in and dragged it back out, her tight walls clenching around his digit as if to try and keep him inside. "You're whining."

Sadie squirmed and rolled her hips, desperate for him.

She didn't even know there was a difference, but apparently Jagger did.

"*Please*, please, please, Jagger." She gasped as his finger pushed inside her again. "I'm- Ah!" Her breath caught on a groan as he hooked his finger right against her G-Spot, the rough pad of his finger eliciting the most delicious sensations through her. *"Begging."*

His teeth nipped at the lace between her thighs while his finger began a 'come hither' motion inside her. "*What* do you want?" He kissed right above where her bundle of nerves were screaming for attention beneath the lace.

"Be a good girl for me. I need you to say it."

A flush ran over Sadie's cheeks, and she thought she was ridiculous for feeling shy in a moment like this, especially after all the things they had done this past week at the bar and over the phone. When she didn't speak immediately, Jagger shoved another finger inside her, and she mewled as she bucked her hips, pushing herself in his face.

She heard him inhale sharply as she felt his nose and mouth pull back from her thrusted pelvis.

"*Fuck*, you smell good," he choked out.

"I want your tongue on me, Wilder."

Sadie was too close to imploding with lust to care about her embarrassment any longer.

"Please put your mouth on my-" She paused, unable to finish the sentence. As much as she'd like to believe she wasn't as much of a good girl as she'd been brought up to be, Sadie still hesitated.

"Come on, baby," Jagger teased and moved the lace to the side with his free hand to hold it out of the way, the wetness on her outer lips tingling as it met the breath that fell from his lips.

"Show me how dirty that mouth can be," he purred while he withdrew his fingers and slid them up her slit before spreading her folds wide with his index and middle finger, exposing her entirely to him. "And I promise to return the favor."

Sadie looked down to find him staring intently at her. His eyes glazed over with barely controlled need, and she finally snapped.

"I want you to fuck my cunt with your tongue," she whispered.

Jagger hummed in approval.

"There you go," he praised. "That wasn't so hard, was it?"

He gave her a cocky wink, and she swore she was going to break free from this damn contraption and ride his face herself. She opened her mouth to tell him as much but found herself letting out a silent scream as his lips wrapped around her engorged clit and sucked hard.

"Jagger!" Sadie gasped when she finally remembered how to speak. He kept his mouth latched onto her pulsing nub as his rough tongue made languid strokes against either side of it.

Sadie's head thrashed against the stocks, and she desperately pulled against her restraints, the clanking of chains only drowned out by her chanting of his name and drawn-out expletives like a filthy mantra. He devoured her, only stopping his assault on her clit to lap at the silky liquid escaping her pussy as he brought her closer and closer to the edge with every brush of his tongue.

"Oh my, God," she cried as her legs started to shake, her thighs trembling, and if she wasn't being held up by the wicked wooden X, she surely would have collapsed by now.

"Fuck, fuck, *fuck*," Sadie practically sobbed, turning her face into her shoulder.

Jagger's teeth grazed along her nub and took the silkiness of her labia between his lips before tugging gently, moaning his encouragement against her heat.

Sadie felt herself being hurdled into oblivion, the intense pleasure of his mouth and the obscene wet noises filling the room too much to handle. She had no idea where he learned to be so good with his damn tongue, but the man deserved a fucking medal. It only took a few more swirls of his tongue to bring her to the edge, and when he angled his head, forcing his tongue into her depths, she unraveled. Her orgasm coated his tongue, which he lapped at hungrily as she spasmed against the wooden X that held her captive to her beautiful dominant.

"Like fucking honey, Sweets. *Christ.*" Jagger moaned against her sensitive flesh before greedily running his tongue along her outer folds, careful not to let a drop go to waste.

"That was so-" Sadie breathed before stopping short, the sound of something outside the door catching her attention.

Jagger's head snapped up, and he quickly pulled the wet lace back over Sadie's pussy that was still throbbing with the aftershocks of her release.

"What the fuck is that?"

He turned his attention to the door, listening intently to what was happening in his office.

"Are you sure it's in here?"

"Yes, he never lets anyone in there."

Jagger was just getting to his feet, steeling for whatever was coming for them and ready to fight when the telltale signs of the lock being picked were heard, and the door swung open.

"Jazlyn?!" Jagger roared as the blonde barged through the door.

"Bianca?!" Sadie gasped simultaneously, seeing the familiar redhead fall in line behind the gang leader.

Jazlyn and Bianca stopped short, clearly not expecting there to be anyone in the room they had just broken into. And most definitely not expecting to stand in the middle of Jagger's playroom.

And with a shackled Sadie Sweetwater breathlessly hanging from a sex contraption, no less.

Jagger moved toward them angrily, and they backed up until Bianca squealed, having crashed into a black iron rack of carefully hung whips, flogs, and paddles of different sizes.

"What are you doing here?" His tone was low and dangerous.

"I was coming for our shit, Wilder. I know you fuckers took it." Jazlyn spat at him, trying to cover up her alarm.

Jagger just looked at her tiredly before scrubbing a hand over his face and gesticulating around him.

"What stash, Jazlyn?" He said in exasperation.

"How many times have I fucking told you we don't do that shit anymore."

"You just have a sex dungeon?" Jazlyn inquired, quirking her eyebrow at Sadie, who glared at her.

Jagger ignored her as his hand slammed against the wall next to Bianca's head when she started to sneak out of the room.

"And you're working for her? Is that why you got a job at my bar? To fucking spy on me?"

Bianca shrugged her shoulders and fully faced him. Jagger could see the bruising under her eyes that were still reflecting the consequences of the broken nose Sadie had given her over the weekend and felt pride swell in him. *Good fucking girl,* he thought.

"I mean, yeah," Bianca admitted and locked eyes with Sadie over his shoulder. "Except pissing off your girlfriend was all me."

Sadie's eyes were dark with rage when she bit out, "Fuck you."

"I'm glad she broke your fucking nose."

Camille's voice rang out from the office before stepping into the room and blowing a low whistle. Her eyes raked over the scene before her, and she crossed her arms. "What's with the sex dungeon, Jag?"

Jagger stepped backward from the crowd in his secret room and moved his body to stand protectively before Sadie.

Who was still tied up.

Shit.

"Can everyone stop calling it that, please?" He begged, rubbing his face with his hands again. "Why are you here, Camille?"

Camille rolled her eyes at him as she grabbed onto Bianca's elbow, looking quite menacing despite her wearing a pair of pink pajamas.

"You called me for backup earlier, remember? Sorry, I'm late. But I got here just in time to help take out the trash again."

"Who're you calling trash, bitch?" Bianca snarled at Camille, trying to break free from her hold.

Camille yanked her towards the door and signaled for Jazlyn to follow. Jazlyn's eyes raked over Sadie's body again, seemingly still aroused by the earlier incident with the same blonde.

Sadie smirked at her and gave her a wink before Camille smacked Jazlyn on the ass to get her attention. "Come on, you too. I'll make sure you get home real safe," Camille whispered in her ear suggestively.

Jagger barely got out a "Thank you" before Jazlyn disappeared back into the office while Camille forcibly removed a rabid Bianca from the sex dungeon. *Fuck.* The playroom.

"I want details tomorrow, Sadie!" Camille yelled over her shoulder as she shut the door behind them, the sound of footsteps and Bianca's whining retreating through the bar.

Sadie was laughing at the absurdity of their situation when Jagger spun to face her. He had the most apologetic look anyone could have mustered as he hurriedly freed her from the device. She breathed a deep sigh of relief, rubbing at her wrists while he unfastened her ankles, running his thumbs along the red marks around them and pushing blood flow back to the area.

"I'm really starting to hate it here," Jagger mumbled, still perched on the ground before her. He was staring at her ankles and shaking his head when Sadie knelt down and grabbed his face in her hands. Her eyes were gentle and warm.

"Jagger Wilder, you love it here. You just hate the interruptions."

She adjusted and moved to stand up, grabbing his hands and helping him to his feet. "And besides, we've really fixed this place up. It's finally making good money; we're not killing ourselves to pay the bills, and I like being here with you."

Jagger wrapped his arms around her, breathing in her scent and nuzzling his face in her hair. "I like you being here with me, too." He dropped a kiss to the top of her head and slid his hands along her spine, pressing her closer.

Everything's better with you here.

Sadie's arms circled his waist, and she smiled against his chest. "I don't think they'll be back again. Not after finding your sex dungeon and walking in on us."

Jagger growled, pressing his fingers into her sides, which elicited a few sharp giggles from Sadie as she squirmed against him. "It's not a sex dungeon."

Sadie pushed against his chest to turn her attention up to his face and pulled on his lower lip with her teeth, running her tongue along it in a sensual swipe. "I know, babe."

She pressed a quick kiss to his mouth. "But it fucking looks like it."

Jagger groaned and dropped his head to rest his forehead against hers. "I'm locking this place up forever. The embarrassment is too great, and I shall never recover."

He knew he was being dramatic, and Sadie told him as much. For such a scary-looking biker boy, he was soft as hell around her, and they both knew it.

When Sadie shivered, signaling she was getting cold from her lack of clothing, Jagger wrapped his jacket around her, and her arms slid into the sleeves easily.

"Let's get you upstairs. I think we've had enough surprises this week to last a lifetime. I just want to get you into bed now," he said as he grabbed her hand.

"I'd really like that," Sadie breathed and started to follow behind him as they left the room.

Jagger laughed, "I didn't mean it like that. I meant to warm you up and let you lay down."

She pressed him into the doorframe as they approached the office, her lips on his neck eager to tease. "Still viable options when you're sinking into me while my legs are wrapped around your waist."

The desperate noise he made in the back of his throat was practically shameful, and he pulled her flush against him, capturing her mouth with his own. She responded quickly to him, craving his touch again after being rudely interrupted.

Jagger deepened the kiss, his tongue creeping past her lips to drive her own tongue wild, breath mingling. When her fingers gripped his inky locks, twisting and pulling them, using the tension to bring him tighter against her, he hoisted her up by her backside. Instinctively, she wrapped her legs around his waist, and all of a sudden, they were in the office, her back slamming into one of the gray-painted walls while he ravaged the skin of her throat with his mouth.

"Jag," Sadie gasped, rolling her hips against him, the evidence of his arousal pressing hard against her as she continued to rut against him. "I need you to take me upstairs."

Jagger's mouth was on her chest now, his tongue sliding under the lace of her bra and drawing a moan from her as his tongue swiped against her erect nipple. "I don't know if I'll make it." He admitted, chuckling at himself and then roughly pulling her breast from the fabric of her bra so he could take the peak in his mouth.

Sadie arched her back against the wall, pushing her hips against his in a maddening rhythm, and her hands clutched his shoulders.

"You can," she encouraged, rolling her hips again.

"FUCK. Sadie, stop fucking moving against me like that, or we're not going anywhere," he pleaded, and he noticed his hands were trembling as they gripped her hips.

"I could always just say my safeword, Jag," she joked, and he let out a dark chuckle, his eyes meeting hers as he looked up from his attention to her chest.

"You don't even have one yet," he growled and thrust against her suddenly, pushing her into the wall again.

Sadie's chin dropped to her chest as she let out a gasp. "I-I do, though.."

Jagger slowly pulled back from her and gave her his full attention, wanting to hear what she had chosen.

"What is it?" He asked and set her down, her feet landing softly on the floor.

Sadie's whole face became a grin as she locked eyes with him.

"Bianca."

Jagger's head whipped back as his whole body was wracked with laughter before replying, "That would definitely force me to stop dead in my tracks."

Sadie grabbed his hand and started tugging him along.

"Well, don't stop now! It's been a week of outrageous foreplay, and after experiencing your tongue tonight, I'm going to lose it if I don't find out how your cock feels, too."

Jagger followed behind Sadie as she quickly dragged him through the bar and couldn't help that his mouth hung open in shock. This was the girl that he had study sessions with in college. The one who moved back to their hometown to help him save his father's business. His best friend, who he'd had a million and one experiences with, and now she's almost naked and hurrying him upstairs.

What a fucking difference a week makes.

"You've got a filthy fucking mouth when you want it, don't you, sweet girl?" He said in awe as her shyness dissipated as he hurried after her.

She tossed her hair over her shoulder and continued to breeze towards his room, briefly turning back to grin at him.

"All the better to suck you off with, my dear," she quipped.

Jagger wasn't sure how she managed to strip him of his clothes so fast the moment they were back in his room, but as her tongue traced the elastic band of his black boxer briefs, he really didn't care.

"You sure you don't want to wait?" Jagger offered, his fingers threading through her hair as she continued to drive him crazy. Her teeth pulled on his waistband before letting go with a *'snap'* as it settled against his hips again.

Jagger let out a chuckle. "I'll take that as a 'no'."

"That was a 'hell no'," Sadie mumbled as she hooked her thumbs in his waistband and pulled them down in one swift motion, his thick erection bobbing in front of her face like a beacon. Jagger didn't have time to step out of them before her lips wrapped around him eagerly.

"Sweets," he hissed as her tongue swirled around the tip before taking the rigid length of him deep inside her, hitting the back of her throat. "Fuck me, you look gorgeous

down there."

Sadie made an appreciative moan and stretched her left hand up to claw her nails quickly down the tattoo of the serpent that covered his hip and thigh.

Jagger's arm shot out behind him to brace against the wall because he was sure he was about to fall over. His other hand reached down to tangle in her hair and guide her as she worked him over with her mouth, her hands gripping his muscular thighs. He couldn't get over how her tongue felt like molten velvet over his throbbing cock, and the twisting motions she was doing with her head were making it feel like it was moving over every inch of him at once.

So, this is what a blow job is supposed to feel like? He wondered, thinking back and not finding one memory of a time this act felt half as good.

Jagger looked down at her, and she slowed her movements to stare up at him through her lashes. Her lips swollen, tears clinging to the corners of her eyes as she pushed herself to her limits. He'd never seen such a sinful sight before, and he groaned out loud because he had felt that way this whole damn week. She was an unbelievable force and he couldn't believe it had taken them this long to figure out they were made for each other.

"Your mouth is so good at that, baby," Jagger managed to choke out, as Sadie did another slow glide of taking him all the way down to her throat again.

Does this siren have a gag reflex? He thought, and his grip on the wall faltered when she hummed in approval at his praises, the vibrations going straight through his groin and into his soul.

Jagger glanced around the room and tried to bring his focus to something - anything else before he shot his load off too soon. The bed was to their left and his chair was to their right and the moon was coming through his windows, making Sadie look like an ethereal cock-sucking goddess.

Fuck.

He straightened on shaky legs to grip her shoulders with his hands. "Sadie, baby, you need to stop," he groaned between clenched teeth. He could feel himself ready to spill into her mouth, and he wanted to wait until he was inside of her.

When she started picking up the pace and moved a hand up to cup his balls firmly, he almost lost his balance and reached over to grasp the chair beside him and the bed. She paused only for a second to allow him to sit in the chair, her mouth never stalling from its task as her face contorted in desire, and she reveled in the precum her ministrations were making him leak out.

His boxers were still wrapped around an ankle, and Sadie tugged it free for him as she sucked him deep again, clutching onto his thighs. Jagger's head slammed back across the top of the chair, and his hand wrapped around the back of her neck. His fingers tangled her blonde hair as he cried out her name. He was so close there was no stopping now.

"I'm gonna lose it, fuck."

His hips jerked and forced his member deeper than it had gone before. Sadie moaned around him and gave an-

other hard suckle, and when her teeth grazed the underside of his cock he stiffened and came crashing through
the galaxy straight into the molten ecstasy that was Sadie
Sweetwater's mouth. He moved his hands to the arms of
the chair and gripped them while spasms rocked his body
in time with the ripples of his release that Sadie hastily
swallowed.

Sadie continued to run her tongue along him gently as
he regained his composure. When he sat up fully, his cock
fell from her lips, and she ran a suggestive fingertip across
the corner of her mouth before winking at him.

"Yum," Sadie said, her eyes twinkling with pride in how
she made him fall apart for her.

Jagger made a strangled sound, his ache to make her
his now insatiable, as he gripped the front of his leather
jacket that she looked so goddamn good in and lifted her
into his lap. Her hands braced against his bare chest, and
he used his grip on the coat to pull her down to him,
their mouths meeting hungrily. He could taste himself on
her lips, and there was something so filthy and animalistic
about it that it made him crave to know what they'd taste
like if his mouth was still full of her orgasm from earlier.

Jagger released the jacket and moved his hands to her
hips, where he gathered the fabric of the black lace of her
panties in his grasp. His mouth moved hungrily against
hers, and he pulled - *hard* - and the fabric shredded,
allowing him access to the apex of her thighs, where he
quickly pushed two long fingers inside her.

Sadie cried out against his mouth, her fingernails biting into his shoulders from the feel of him inside her again,

and then let out a pitiful sob as they pulled out just as quickly.

She pulled back to ask, "Why did you stop?"

Jagger held his fingers up to her lips, the digits glistening with her arousal. "Suck."

The heat in his eyes took her breath away, and she obeyed, taking them in her mouth and sucking her juices off his fingers. Her tongue lapped around each one, and her teeth clanked against the rings on his hand. Jagger hadn't even entirely removed them from her mouth before kissing her deeply, his tongue dancing with her own. The combination of them - him salty and her sweet - was addictive. The most incredible drug he could have imagined.

And he spent his life around drugs. He would know.

He let out a groan, and when she mimicked his sounds on her own, he knew she felt the same way.

Sadie shifted on top of him and dragged her wet folds along his cock, the tip brushing against her clit. He was still raging hard, and she knew she wouldn't have to wait long to have him inside of her.

"Jagger," she whispered, pulling back to look at him, her blonde waves framing her face. "I know these couple days have seemed intense and out of nowhere, but I've always had feelings for you."

"Me too," Jagger swallowed and visibly shifted gears in his mind to try and concentrate on what she was saying and not on how close he was to being inside of her. "You're the most glorious specimen of a woman in the world, and I'm not blind. I've always seen you for what you are. Mine."

Even though it was dark in his room, illuminated only by the moon and streetlight outside his window, he could still see a blush creep over her cheeks.

"I just need you to know that this isn't some rebound from Travis or something. I liked you before I dated him. I just started to become painfully aware that I couldn't be with him when I was still thinking about you. Not that he needed me for anything but my good reputation."

Sadie lifted herself up and started to sink down on him slowly, their eyes locked.

Jagger inhaled sharply, and his fingers dug into her hips, scraps of lace still tangled across the top of her right thigh.

"This is everything I've ever wanted, Sweets."

His own confession fueled Sadie, and she took him all the way inside her.

"Wow."

"Holy fuck."

They spoke simultaneously, adjusting to the feeling of being fully joined.

Sadie started moving almost immediately, her thighs straining as she brought herself up and down on him. Jagger leaned forward to press kisses along her jawline as he assisted her in her movements.

"As much as I love you in my jacket, *why the fuck is it still on* ?" He demanded to know as he started to push it off her shoulders while his mouth ravaged her neck and collarbone.

Sadie tilted her head back to give her more access and gasped, "No idea." She let go of him long enough to throw the jacket on the floor. His hands moved over her spine as he blindly grasped the hooks of her bra. She caught his lips with hers again, and they kissed while she continued to ride him, angling her hips to brush the tip of his cock with each thrust. After the third hook he unfastened, he cursed as he saw the bra remain in place.

Jagger tore his mouth away from hers to ask, "What the fuck is wrong with this thing?"

Sadie laughed at his frustration and leaned down to kiss his neck as he fumbled with the hooks. "It has six hooks, I think, or seven. It's like a little corset bra."

Jagger scoffed, sounding offended that the article of clothing dared to be so difficult to remove when he thought he was an expert bra remover at this point in his life. His hands moved to the front, where he tore it open, exposing her breasts and nipples to his searching mouth. "That's so much better," he mumbled between taking turns kissing her breast and swirling his tongue around her pink nipple.

"Jagger! What the hell?!" Sadie huffed and stilled her motions, "You can't just rip all my shit off. You need -"

Jagger bit softly at the underside of her breast and lifted her hips up, leaving just the tip of his cock inside her while she hovered over his lap. "I absolutely can. And why do you care?"

He thrust up hard inside her, keeping his hold on her hips in elevation so he now had control of the movements, pushing into her over and over at an increasing speed.

"How many shopping trips have I gone on with you over the years?" He pointed out between thrusts. "Oh no, I must add lingerie shopping to our outings now? What-ever will I do?" He rolled his eyes, clearly okay with it.

"Just shut up and let me ride you like that bike you love so much," Sadie growled down at him.

Jagger took her in. Wild blonde hair tangled past her shoulders, and perky breasts bounced in time with each push of his cock.

"You know. I'm trying real hard here not to take you to the bed and fuck you into the mattress, but you're making it really, really hard."

"It's already hard," she giggled as she raked her nails down his chest, and Jagger bit her shoulder, making her keen into him.

"You think you're so cute," he chided as he stood and carried her to the bed. Her squeal of delight echoed in the room as her back hit the mattress and her legs curled around his waist.

"I think you think I'm cute," she teased and licked his pulse point, dragging her tongue up before nipping his earlobe.

"Now destroy this pussy, Wilder."

"Yes, darling."

Jagger was still standing off the side of the bed, his hands under her hips, holding her pelvis to him as he slammed into her.

"Do you know how bad I've wanted to do this with you?" He moaned, taking pleasure in her gasps as she writhed beneath him.

"Tell me," she pleaded, needing his delicious words to stroke the other part inside of her that worked in tandem with the G-spot he was hitting.

"Since the first day I saw you smile at me in class," Jagger admitted, his movements becoming erratic as he teetered on the edge. He reached between them to rub circles on her aching clit with the pad of his thumb as he continued to pump into her. "I only wanted to grab your ponytail and bend you over the desk."

Sadie's back curled off the bed, the combination of his cock and attention to her clit driving her absolutely wild.

"Oh, god, Jag," she cried, "More. I need more." She sobbed, and her arms wrapped around his shoulders, bringing him closer to her.

"I want every fucking thing with you."

He slapped her clit, and stars shot across her vision.

"I want all this shit life has to offer if it's with you."

The stark contrast of his rough and dirty fucking mixed with his sweet words had Sadie spiraling, and all of a sudden, she was coming hard around his cock. Her walls clenched him tight, and before she realized what was happening, she felt liquid gush around her thighs from her pussy - more than she'd ever had before. Her blue eyes looked black, and she stared at Jagger's face in shock as she continued squirting. His eyes never left her as he made quick deep thrusts and frantically rubbed four digits in a salute against her clit to elongate her climax.

Sadie sobbed his name as her fingers clawed his back, her orgasm tearing through her like a wildfire that started in her heart and ended with their joined bodies.

"I love you," she chanted repeatedly, and Jagger stilled above her. Her confession of love mixed with her milking his cock through her release had him trembling as he finally let go and spilled himself inside her. Her pussy greedily pulled on him, willing each drop of cum to find a home in her womb. Carefully, he pulled his hand from between their bodies to grip her face.

"I've *always* loved you, Sadie Sweetwater."

With that, he leaned forward and gently kissed her lips, to which she returned. She ran her fingers through his hair, lightly raking his scalp with her nails.

Her body was still shaking with emotion and after-shocks as Jagger moved his mouth down her body to her swollen center. His eyes raked over the scene in front of him, both of their orgasms blending together as they peeked through her swollen pink pussy lips and flowed onto her thighs and the bed. The blue of his eyes was almost gone, and his pupils were blown wide when he looked up at her. Sadie's brow furrowed as she looked down at him in confusion and grinned.

"What are you doing down there?" Sadie asked, propping herself up on her elbows.

He shrugged and held her gaze as he leaned forward.

"You know I'm always hungry."

Sadie opened her mouth to speak, but his mouth was already on her, lapping up their juices and cursing against her sensitive flesh. "Fuck. Oh my, god."

He groaned and ran his tongue up her slit greedily, lavishing her with attentiveness. "I could get used to this."

Sadie bucked her hips under him as another orgasm quickly tore through. "*Jag!* Stop!" She panted, but he only let up after she came again with his name on her tongue and her sweet release on his.

Jagger lifted his head to give her a lopsided smile, her shine still coating his chin. "Goddamn, baby. I could do this all night."

Sadie rolled her eyes, placed a foot against his shoulder, and kicked gently. Jagger laughed as he toppled backward onto the floor, looking like a Greek god with the sweat gleaming off his muscled body.

"Give a girl a break for a minute. Jesus," she muttered, still trying to collect herself. She watched as he sat back up, reached out to grab her knees, and quickly shut them with a warning look.

Jagger laughed again and used her knees as leverage to stand up. "I'll leave you alone for now, but I've waited too damn long for this, so don't expect me to wait patiently."

She felt the same and moved entirely onto the bed, kicking the top sheets off that they had made a mess of while Jagger grabbed a warm wet washcloth from the bathroom.

"You okay?" He asked as he tenderly cleaned the space between her legs and her thighs.

Sadie nodded. "Yeah, just a little overwhelmed."

Jagger crawled onto the bed with an extra blanket after tossing the washcloth in the laundry bin and pulled her close to him, wrapping an arm around her waist. Sadie pulled the blanket around them when he whispered, "I am too. In a good way, though."

"In a good way," Sadie agreed.

"I meant what I said, Sadie," Jagger whispered against her hair.

"I did, too," Sadie said quietly. "So what do we do now?"

She could hear the smile in his voice even though she couldn't see it. "Now we close the bar down for the week and stay in this bed."

Sadie chuckled and gently slapped his arm before settling deeply into the covers. "You cannot close the bar down for a whole week. And I have to work with my mom during the day anyway, so you'd be stuck up here alone."

"Ugh, Karen Sweetwater. I wonder how she'll handle this news," he said dryly, knowing how much Karen disliked him. She made sure to make him aware of it every chance.

Sadie rubbed her hands over her face tiredly. "It will be bad, but she'll get over it." She peeked at him from between her fingers, still held to her face. "But I meant, what are we going to do about... us?"

Jagger leaned over her, propping himself up on his elbow and kissing her nose. "You're always going to be my best friend. That's never going to change. The only different thing is now we have mind-blowing sex whenever we want."

Sadie pinched the bridge of her nose with her fingers in frustration, but she still had a smile on her lips.

Jagger kissed her mouth this time, and she leaned into him. They moved their mouths lazily, and when he pulled away, his hair hung in front of his face, making him look just like the young version of him she had met in college.

"Sadie," he whispered, locking eyes. "We will figure it out the same way we do everything. Together."

Sadie knew he meant it. There was no doubt in her mind.

And when she responded in kind, Jagger knew she meant it, too.

"Together."

Six months.

Six months is all it took for Sadie and Jagger to go from friends to lovers to living together.

The Serpent Pit was bringing in quite a crowd as of late, and the Dregs have yet to be around to bother anyone. They are likely too embarrassed to show their faces since they got their asses handed to them. Jagger's dad, Warren, has officially left the bar to him in his absence but has promised to visit for Christmas. He has also pledged to dole out any other odd jobs to Lethal Lenny and leave Jagger out of it. Jagger got two final roses added to the sleeve on his arm after that call, and when Sadie asked him again what they meant, he told her the truth - that they were in remembrance of the people he had killed when he ran jobs for the Rebels.

Jagger had collapsed into the chair beside his bed with his head in his hands after his confession and waited for her to leave. Sadie simply crawled into his lap and held him until he believed she'd stay.

Sadie continued to bartend on the weekends, seeing as how her boyfriend has to manage the bar anyway, so she might as well help out. During the week, she works full time with her mom and has been enjoying the new freedom of running it herself. Her mother, Karen, decided after a massive fight with her daughter that it was best she take a smaller role in helping with the paper and moved closer to her other daughter, Fiona, to help and spend more time with her grandchildren. The fight had been a necessity; Sadie spoke of how much Karen pressured her to be perfect and that it was causing her to make bad choices for herself to make her happy. Bad decisions like Travis. Karen tried to convince her that she was making a terrible mistake being with "trash from the Southside of Central," but seeing how that "trash" was her best friend and now boyfriend, Karen finally got that slap in the face she deserved. It snapped her out of her controlling haze and made her realize how unfair she had been, which inevitably caused a new chain of events in their lives.

Karen plans to host Christmas for everyone this year since she's still living in the area.

With their past and parents out of the way, it's been a whirlwind as Jagger and Sadie get used to these new dynamics. But they have enjoyed the learning curve - and curves of each other's bodies while they figure it out.

Jagger has a meeting with a publishing house in New York next week about the novel he's been working on since college, and they are counting on their blessings to have made it this far. Sadie gave up the lease on her apartment a month after she and Jagger started seeing each other and moved in above the bar with him. Jagger tried to convince her that they should find a different place together, but she insisted that this would be better until they were more financially stable and could afford a place to move their playroom. She made it very clear that the playroom was as vital to her as it was to him, and he reluctantly agreed to stay at the Serpent Pit until they had some more money saved up or things worked out for his book.

And now, Jagger has some good news to share.

And good news like this calls for a celebration, so he is more than eager to clear out the bar this Sunday evening and spend some much-needed time in his playroom with his live-in girlfriend.

"Everyone out?" Sadie asked, a grin playing on her lips as she finished wiping off the last liquor bottles behind the bar.

Jagger slipped the large bolt in place on the front doors and turned to grin at her. He took long strides to get to her behind the bar, looking very eager as he picked her up from behind, causing her to let out a sound of surprise as she dropped her dishcloth on the ground.

"All clear," he whispered in her ear as he hugged her from behind after setting her back down so her feet were on the ground again.

Sadie turned in his arms and pressed a hard kiss to his mouth before pushing against his chest and backing out of his arms. She reached for a bottle of Jameson Whiskey, poured a four-count into her mouth, and pushed Jagger onto his knees before her. Jagger tilted his head back and let Sadie open his mouth by hooking her thumb over his bottom teeth. Jagger was known to be the dominant in their relationship, but fuck did he love when she did shit like this.

Leaning forward, Sadie let the whiskey drip from her lips into his awaiting mouth, eliciting a dark moan from his chest. After swallowing, Jagger reached out to grab her, but she stepped away again. She lifted her tight white Serpent Pit crop top shirt over her head as she walked backward toward the office and tossed it to the floor before his feet.

"So, that means I can finally get out of these clothes? It's been such a long, hard day." Sadie winked as her hands went to work unbuttoning her tight jean shorts.

Jagger audibly groaned as his left hand shot out to grip the bar top, and he got to his feet. His eyes were glued to her shapely legs as she hooked her thumbs in the waistband of her panties and shorts before pushing them to the ground and stepping out of them. "Jesus, baby."

With just her red lace bra left, she paused to bend over to take off her motorcycle boots, aware that her breasts threatened to spill out of her cups as she did so.

"Leave them on!" Jagger yelled as he grabbed something Sadie couldn't see from under the bar top. He shoved it in his pocket and made his way toward her. His eyes were lustful, and Sadie's breath caught in her throat as she straightened. She could only imagine what was hidden in his pocket and what pleasure it would bring forth during their play.

"Yes, sir," she whispered.

Sadie knew he was beyond ready to have his way with her, but she wanted to continue teasing him for as long as possible. She reached behind her to unclasp her bra, and when he was a few feet in front of her, she whipped it at his head and laughed as he struggled to unwrap it from his head. She could hear him cursing as she ran into the office.

"Sadie! You're going to regret that!" He shouted as she heard his heavy footsteps on the wood floors making their way to the office. He stopped at the office doorway and casually leaned against the frame. His eyes locked with hers as she pressed her back against the door to their playroom. Their playroom. God, that had such a good ring to it.

Casually, Jagger dangled the red lacy bra from his index finger.

"You think you're funny?"

Sadie's voice shook with desire and excitement when she drawled, "Hi-*larious.*"

Jagger chuckled and dropped the bra to the floor. He retrieved the key from his desk and planted himself before her. He was close enough that she could feel the heat of his chest against her own, and she arched her back off the door to push her breasts against him. She let out a small gasp as his left hand braced against the door, and he leaned down to tug on her bottom lip with his teeth.

"You better behave, darling," he mumbled against her mouth before trailing kisses down her jaw.

Sadie could hear the critical jingle against the lock as his right hand blindly tried to unlock the door.

"Or what, tough guy?" She teased and arched into him again, pulling a low growl from his throat that tickled the skin of her neck.

"Or you won't be able to walk for a week," he said as she heard the lock click open behind her.

She grabbed his face in her hands and kissed him again, their tongues coming together in a familiar dance. This time, it was slow and sensual, her tongue then tracing along his lower lip. "Promises, promises."

In one swift movement, he moved her to the side so he could swing the door open and bit her shoulder. Hard.

Sadie yelled at the sudden pain and whimpered as he licked the mark with his tongue.

"Get over to the table. Bend over, grab the ropes, and get ready for me. We will start with your lashings."

Sadie hurried over to the long black leather-bound table in the center of the room and stretched her torso along its length, extending her arms across the expanse to grab the two rope handles bolted to the sides. She made sure to spread her legs as she gazed over her shoulder at him, aware of how her folds were slick already with want as the air hit her center and forced a shiver through her body.

Jagger was stripping his black T-shirt off as he moved along the room, eyes taking in his many choices. She watched as he picked up a black and red leather cat-o-nine tails from the rack behind her. It was a new addition, something that reminded him of the time she danced at the club in her red dress.

They had been so busy that they hadn't played and couldn't try it out yet. They were waiting for a special occasion.

Sadie quickly looked down at the table and took a deep breath. She had had plenty of spankings before, but they were usually with his hand, sometimes a tiny paddle or a riding crop. But she was anxious to try this one. She was always anxious to try anything with him.

"So, I take it we are celebrating because your phone call with the publisher went well the other day?" she whispered against the table, her chin resting on it lightly.

Suddenly, Sadie felt his finger run down the length of her spine, and she sighed at his presence behind her.

"Very," Jagger replied and continued trailing his fingers down the cleft of her ass and down through her nether lips.

Sadie drew in a sharp breath and made a sound of protest when he pulled his finger away.

"I warned you that you would regret teasing me earlier."

She could feel the warmth of his breath against her as his lips began following the trail of his finger just moments ago. His hands gripped her waist tightly, and she could feel the leather-bound tails tickling her side from where they dangled from his right palm against her while he held it. When he had to drop onto his knees to continue his exploration, she couldn't stop trembling when he spoke again.

"Safe word?" He asked as his mouth hovered against her slit.

Sadie's hands tightened on the ropes as she grinned. "Bianca."

Jagger let out a dark chuckle, "Good girl."

And before she could even brace herself, he was sucking hard on her clit, the tip of his tongue running along it as the blood rushed to the area and pulled a shout from her throat. He only lingered for a few seconds before pulling away and standing again, the hilt of the cat-o-nine tails gripped tight in his right hand.

"Jaggie," Sadie whined and wiggled her ass in his direction.

"If you stopped being a brat for two minutes, I wouldn't have to punish you so much," he laughed and lightly kicked one of her boots with his own.

Sadie looked over her shoulder at him, a sly smile on her lips. "If you didn't have reasons to punish me, though, we'd have no reason to use the sex dungeon, babe."

His eyes narrowed at her. "True. I like all the things your mouth does. Seems like it's driving me crazy whether you're speaking or sucking me off with it."

Sadie winked at him for good measure, and his left hand gently grabbed the back of her head and forced her to turn it forward.

"Face forward. You know the rules. Don't make me get the blindfold already." Jagger instructed before releasing his hold on her. He smoothed her long hair over her shoulder so it hung over the side of the table and out of the way before stepping back.

"Yes, sir."

"Good girl." Jagger brought his left hand back to her left hip as he dragged the tails against her lower back. "How many months have we been fucking now?"

"Six," she chirped happily.

"Goddamn right, it's six. The best six months of my life. I'll lash you six times, and you'll count each time, or I start from the beginning. Understood?"

"Mmm, yes." Sadie moaned, the thought making her wild already.

"Yes, what?" Jagger demanded as he brought his left hand down upon her ass sharply.

"Yes, sir!" She gasped.

"*Fuck.* Okay."

Sadie heard him shuffle slightly behind her and knew he was running a hand through his hair the way he always did when flustered.

"Here goes, baby. Tell me if it's too much."

Crack.

The ropes creaked as Sadie pulled against them while she groaned out, "One." The sting of the tails against her ass shot through her like lightning, sparking her nerves with the new sensation.

Crack.

"Shit!" Sadie cried and bit her bottom lip. "Two."

The ends of a few tails managed to hit her center, causing an intense pleasure to pool between her thighs.

Crack.

"Th- *three* !" She gasped, swallowing hard and trying to compose herself.

"You're so good for me, my sweet, sweet girl. Hang in there; you're doing a beautiful job."

Sadie preened at his praise and raised onto the balls of her feet, lifting her bottom up to him by a few inches more, inviting him to continue. Instead, she felt his tongue graze over the red welts that were already forming on her backside.

"I feel like I'm the one being punished right now. You're fucking dripping onto the floor, and all I want is to grab your hair and screw your perfect pussy." Jagger's voice sounded strained, and Sadie could tell he couldn't wait until he lost it.

Jagger moved his left hand down the swell of her hip and in between her folds, where he quickly slipped two fingers inside her. The feeling of his fingertips against her G-spot was exquisite, but it was the feeling of the tails being brought down again with his other hand mixed with his ministrations that had her choking on her own oxygen.

Crack.

"Four," she sobbed and rested her forehead against the table. Sadie felt him crook his fingers against her walls, and she whispered his name. She could feel herself tightening around his digits as an orgasm already threatened to tear through her body.

"*So close*, baby. You're so close; I can feel it. Hold on a little longer, and I'll give you what you want. Don't cum yet." His voice was lower now, and Sadie tried to pull herself back from the edge as best as possible.

Jagger waited until he saw her nod her head 'yes' against the table before drawing his arm back along with the fingers he had inside her and bringing the tails against her red ass again.

Crack.

Right when she arched her back from the bite of the lash, he plunged the fingers in deep and started pumping them quick and hard inside her; the sound of her juices flooding around his hand and falling onto the floor would have embarrassed her if she could think about anything else besides chasing an earth-shattering release.

"Please," Sadie panted and twisted the ropes in her palms, knuckling white. "Wilder, *fuck*!"

"What number are we on, Sadie? Don't stop counting, or I will make you go back to the beginning," Jagger warned but didn't lose momentum with his fingers.

"Jesus, Jag. I'm trying." Sadie bit out. "You're kind of distracting me. Five."

"Good girl. Now, I want you to tell me right when you're about to cum. Then I'll give you your final lashing." She could hear the way he was out of breath, just like her, and she squeezed her eyes shut against the tears that threatened to spill from the intensity of it all. Her ass was on fire, but it only heightened the pleasure as flames of another kind swept through her core as she rocked back onto his fingers while he pumped them frantically inside her.

"Oh, shit! Right *there*, Jag. I'm-I'm going to - "

Crack.

Sadie swore she left her body as the tails came into contact between her thighs. She had been anticipating them on her backside once more, but Jagger had swiped the tails up between her legs to clash against her clit, and she was done for.

"Six!" Sadie screamed as the pain and pleasure mixed together in an orchestrated moment of climax, the waves crashing harder with each push of his fingers against her pulsating walls.

"Come on, Sweets. Let go. Let it all go for me."

Rather than slow down his movements while she cursed under her breath and writhed on the table, Jagger only moved deeper and faster, slapping his drenched palm against her as she gushed more than ever before, his fingers rough and rugged inside her.

"Oh my, *God*. Jagger. *Jagger. Jagger*. FUCK. *Jag!*" She sobbed his name as the splash of her insane orgasm slowed to a trickle down her legs and pooled down into her drenched boots. After a few final thrusts of his fingers, he gingerly pulled them out, and she could hear him sucking on them behind her.

Sadie's eyes met his over her shoulder as she regarded the filthy scene and felt a new wave of need pool in her belly.

"My favorite flavor," he grinned at her even as she rolled her eyes at him.

Carefully and slowly, she released the ropes as she braced herself on the table. When she winced as she straightened, Jagger was fast to check her over. He quickly grabbed a bottle of water from the mini-fridge at the corner of the room and a fresh white rag from on top. Pouring half the bottle of cold water onto the rag, he carefully held it to the swollen globes of her ass.

Sadie sighed as the cold compress took the sting out, and her shoulders relaxed. She made a face as the boots made a 'squishing' noise when she adjusted, and he chuckled as she unzipped and kicked them off her feet.

"Thank you," she whispered, placing her hand over his as it lightly swept over her skin. As she tried to look behind her, she could see only welts and no bruising. The skin was all intact, and there was no bleeding, so the aftercare was pretty minimal, at least.

Which was great, considering they were far from done.

Sadie smiled up at him, her mouth pink and supple, and Jagger couldn't resist the urge to kiss it after he finished securing the wrist restraints to the wall above the red chaise lounge she had brought home after a fantastic weekend of tips at the bar last week.

"How did you even get that here?" He asked incredulously as he gestured to the piece of furniture. The red velvet lounger looked way too upscale, sitting in the middle of the Serpent Pit early on a Sunday morning.

"The guy I bought it from was nice enough to drive it over for me," Sadie smirked.

Jagger sighed, "I'm sure he was more than eager to help you."

"Yep! That's why when I thanked him, I told him how excited I was to have my boyfriend fuck me on it as soon as possible," she said cheekily as she sat on it and made a sexy pose as she stretched on top of it.

"Paint me like one of your French girls, Jack."

Jagger rolled his eyes, but he couldn't keep the grin that spread across his lips. "I'd like to do much more than paint you on that thing."

Sadie slipped a hand into the front pocket of her jeans and raised an eyebrow at him. "Oh, yeah? Tell me all about it."

Jagger glanced at the clock and knew they had exactly twenty minutes to open the bar. Plenty of time to get her off and drag the new addition to the playroom.

He dropped to his knees behind her on the bar's hardwood floor and pressed his lips to the skin above the waistband of her jeans.

"You got it, Rose."

"I knew it would fit perfectly here in the corner. How are the new links holding up?" Sadie cocked her head back and yanked on her wrist cuffs that were hooked into the comprehensive 'O' links that Jagger bracketed to the wall above it earlier that week.

Jagger reached above her head and jangled them a bit, staring down at her. "Seems fine, but we should test them out to be sure."

Sadie nodded eagerly, eyes bright. "Absolutely."

Jagger trailed his hands down the length of her arms as he sat beside her form that was lying on the couch and deftly started tickling her underarms, eliciting a shriek as she started jerking around in laughter.

"They seem pretty good. We might not need to do any more testing," he teased, but he did pull his hands back and allow her to collapse against the cushions, her flushed face complementing the red velvet beneath her.

"You're the worst," she said breathlessly, but her glare wasn't convincing, and her laughter was still bubbling in her chest.

Jagger kissed the bridge of her nose lightly. "And yet, you tell me I'm the best you've ever had."

He barely stood up in time to miss the swift kick of her leg and let out a chuckle. "So feisty tonight."

"If you don't come over here and fuck me, I promise 'feisty' will be an understatement," Sadie growled, and he sidestepped her leg, swinging towards him again.

"Watch it, you minx," he growled and grabbed her ankle before it could connect with his crotch. "I'm gonna need that for later."

"Jagger!" Sadie snapped impatiently.

He placed her leg back onto the lounger and grabbed a plain black satin blindfold off the wall beside him. He gazed down into her eyes as he started slipping the elastic around her head's crown.

"See you on the other side," Jagger whispered before settling the blindfold above her cheekbones.

With her vision officially compromised for the time being, Jagger allowed himself a moment to collect himself. He'd been rock hard since he'd chased her into the office an hour ago, and his erection was pressing painfully against his zipper. But it wasn't just his lust that was causing him to be anxious.

God, I hope this goes okay.

He quickly went about the room, gathered the other few items he wanted to use that night, and dug something out of his pocket from earlier to place beside them. Jagger was lost in thought, looking at a set of nipple clamps in his hands, when her voice broke through his haze.

"Are you okay?" Sadie asked sincerely. He normally didn't hesitate with her in the room, but the silence was making her nervous.

Jagger released a sharp breath and straightened his shoulders, ready to continue.

"Perfect. Just daydreaming about you," he replied, walking back towards her.

"Why are you daydreaming? I'm right here," she said as she smiled and moved her head in the direction of his steps.

"I was thinking about how good you would look in these."

Her gasp filled the room as he settled the silver clamps to fit tight over the buds of her breasts.

Jagger loved all the different noises he could get her to make. When he reached beside him to grab the matchbox and light the little red candle he had brought over, her shuddering moan at the sound was like hearing his favorite song on the radio in the middle of the night.

"Really?" She squealed as she bent her knees on the chaise lounge and planted her feet. Whether for comfort or to steel herself for what was coming next, who knew?

"You said you wanted to try it. I thought tonight could be filled with a few firsts."

Jagger picked up the candle and moved himself to settle beside her. He kept his clothes on to force himself to get her to cum at least one more time before he plunged into her. The candle hovered above her stomach, and he grabbed the silver chain that dangled between her breasts from the clamps on her nipples with his free hand. As he watched her chest rise and fall with her shallow breaths, he slowly began dripping the wax above her navel.

"Mmmff!" Sadie cried as she sucked in a breath.

Jagger tugged on the clamps and pulled another luscious noise from her throat. "Too much?"

Sadie shook her head, "*No.*"

Jagger grew a little bolder and drizzled the wax up her sternum and across her left breast, and she squirmed beneath him. She felt something cold against her lips when he tugged on her chain.

"Bite it," Jagger commanded, sliding the chain between her teeth. Her nipples were pulled taut along with her breasts, and she had to drop her chin to her chest so she could keep it from being pulled out of her mouth.

"I want to fuck you so bad, baby. You know that, don't you?" His voice was heavy with need, and it was a miracle he could still continue with their game.

Drip.

Drip.

Drip.

More red wax painted itself across her breasts until she thrust her hips in his direction, desperate for him.

He smirked down at her, an absolute sight stretched out for him. The red wax was hardening against her skin, and he brought the candle lower until he could drip some across the apex of her thighs, right above her glistening folds.

"Damn, I love it, Jag," Sadie praised him, and the chain fell from her lips to settle between her breasts again as he set the candle down on the table beside them once more. "My whole cunt is aching for you. Can you tell?"

Jagger swallowed hard, her words causing him to lose himself, but he still took the time to delicately peel off the wax from her skin before quickly grabbing something off the table. Then he was kneeling between her legs and gripping the inside of her thighs roughly. He lifted her legs over his shoulder and kissed the soft skin right above her slit.

"Tell me how bad you want my tongue on you."

"So bad," Sadie whispered as she shivered in anticipation.

Jagger slapped the length of his fingers across her clit, and she arched off the couch with a gasp.

"Speak up."

"Holy shit. I want your tongue on my clit.. I want you to make me cum with your sexy fucking mouth," she practically yelled, and he slapped her pussy again.

"Good girl."

And then his mouth was on her heat, licking languidly up and down her glistening slit. She twisted in her shackles and panted his name, pressing her hips into his face. Jagger moved his hands under her to grip her ass as he devoured her like a man starved. He sucked her clit between his lips and began flicking the tip of his tongue along it rapidly, knowing it would drive her crazy.

"Too much! It's too - ungh!" Sadie cried and tried to pull back, but she was powerless against him. Just when she was about to cum, he pulled his mouth away and grabbed the large vibrating wand he quickly plugged into the wall.

"Where did you go?" She whined and pouted.

"I'm right here, baby," he whispered as he held the head of the wand to her clit.

"Jag?" Sadie questioned when she felt the cool object against her center.

Jagger repositioned himself between her legs and darted his tongue inside her pussy, pressing into her opening.

"Damn, this pussy tastes so fucking good. I can never get enough of you on my tongue. Now be my good fucking girl, and cum all over my face."

Sadie's mouth dropped from shock at his words, but she absolutely loved it.

Jagger flipped on the vibrations to the highest setting, not giving her a chance to warm up as he hungrily pushed his tongue inside her, licking at her walls and drinking in her arousal each time.

Sadie was screaming from the intensity of his attention. The vibrator worked against her clit thoroughly, and his tongue moved in tandem to bring her to an earth-shattering finish. When she started to bear down on his tongue, he withdrew it and sat up to watch her face as he pressed the wand harder against her center. When Jagger heard her gasp his name and her head reel back, he grabbed the chain and yanked the clamps off her nipples. The sudden pinch as the clamps popped off threw her over the edge, and she frantically grinded against the vibrator as the shocks of her orgasm tore through her.

Unable to resist, Jagger stared at her as her breathing slowed before he turned off the wand and laid it gently on the floor beside them. He quietly picked up the small red box next to his hip on the couch before taking out something small and leaning over her. He pressed a deep kiss to her mouth, their tongues massaging one another through her haze, and he gingerly slipped something onto one of her fingers above her head.

Sadie was so overcome with her orgasm and the way he was kissing her that she almost didn't notice him slipping something onto her finger.

Almost.

"Take my blindfold off."

"Sweets- "

"Now."

Jagger sighed as he slipped the blindfold off and panicked a little, wondering if he should have done this differently. Take her out to a nice dinner. Waited until the holidays when their families were together. Anything.

Sadie blinked up at him and tried to get her eyes to adjust to the lights, even though they were dim. She looked calm but still shaken from her recent orgasm, and she was wringing her fingers together, trying to feel the object that now adorned one of them.

"The cuffs, too," she whispered.

Still holding her gaze, he reached up, took out her right hand, and gently released her left.

Sadie rushed to sit up and stared at the large diamond ring on her finger. It was beautiful, with at least a carat in the middle of the princess cut and dozens of smaller ones around it in a halo around the band.

"Oh, my god," Sadie breathed, holding it up to her face.

"I know this was probably not the best time to do this, but I didn't want to wait anymore," Jagger confessed, the words rushing quickly from his lips as he grabbed her hands in his.

"It's beautiful. And huge. Like, how can we afford this 'huge'?"

Jagger allowed himself a small smile at how she had said 'we'.

"I wasn't entirely honest when I told you about the meeting with the publishing house. They weren't thinking about taking on my book. They already bought it. They sent my advance this week, and I went right out and bought this ring."

"Jagger, that's incredible! You worked so hard on that manuscript. I'm so proud of you. And mad! How did you not tell me until now?" Sadie was clutching onto Jagger's hands as she leaned forward. She was still naked, he still fully clothed in his signature jeans and a black t-shirt.

"I wanted to get through tonight first," he grinned.

Sadie looked down at the hand where her ring sparkled on her finger. "Oh."

"I know it seems a little fast, but we've known each other for years. We've both been friends, worked together, lived together, have incredible sex, and accept each other for who we really are." Jagger paused to rest his forehead against hers as he looked down at her hand with her.

"You make the world around me feel calm. You make the world stop spinning and breathe air into my lungs whenever I see you enter a room. I can't imagine this life without your smart mouth, beauty, and support. Please say yes."

Sadie looked up at him through her lashes, now wet with tears. Her voice was innocent when she spoke next, "If I say 'yes', are you finally gonna have sex with me tonight?"

Jagger's mouth hung open as he stared back at her. "What?"

Sadie laughed and pressed her mouth to his in a sweet kiss. She loved it when she could render him speechless, and this was still as good a time as any.

After a few more kisses, she pulled away and whispered, "Yes, sir."

"Thank god, baby."

Jagger couldn't hold back anymore; the emotion of the evening coursing through him, and in a flash, he was out of his clothes and kneeling between her thighs on the lounge.

"Jag?" Sadie whispered, her eyes still glistening with moisture. "I love you."

Jagger's hands tensed on her hips as the tip of his cock pressed against her entrance.

"I love you, too. So much. Let me show you."

Sadie nodded her head and pulled him down for a searing kiss as he pushed inside her. He wanted to take it slow, but the warm velvet of her pussy had him pounding into her in seconds.

"How the fuck are you so tight all the time?" He groaned before dropping his head to rest in the crook of her neck. "Fuck, Sweets."

"Because my body was made for you, Wilder." She growled back and lifted her hips to meet his thrusts.

"I'm not gonna last long at all. I've been on the edge since I strapped you on here," Jagger admitted as his hands carded through Sadie's hair while his teeth nipped at her throat.

"It's okay; you have our whole lives to make it up to me." She moaned and scratched her nails down his back, trying to pull him even closer to her.

"Fuck, yes, I do," he groaned as he pulled his head up to look at her. "You're mine. Say it."

"I'm yours," Sadie cried, her walls tightening around his shaft as he hit that spot deep inside of her over and over again. "I've always been yours."

Sadie grabbed his left hand and placed it around her throat, her subtle gesture granting him permission to apply pressure. They both knew that the slight restriction of oxygen helped her over the edge, and he was more than happy to oblige.

When she convulsed around him, her pussy fluttering around his cock, he spilled into her with a groan that sounded like it had been yanked from his core. While he throbbed inside her, emptying everything he had, she held him close. The sounds of their heavy breathing filled the room until Sadie started giggling beneath him.

"What's so funny?" Jagger mumbled against her breast, his eyes still closed as he tried to catch his breath.

Sadie stroked her fingers through his hair a few times before she answered. "You know we'll have to make up an engagement story. People will ask how you did it, and I don't think we can tell them."

I did not think this through.

"We can tell Camille." Jagger offered lamely.

"True, but I'm not telling this story to our parents at Christmas," Sadie said in exasperation.

"Fine." Jagger grinned. "We can tell them I did it at a nice restaurant. Music, roses, a crowd of strangers staring at us. You know, shit that Karen would love."

"Oh, god," Sadie laughed, "You're right; she'd love it." Completely sated and spent, she yawned and hugged Jagger tighter. When he went to remove himself from her, she groaned in protest. They always cleaned up and went to bed after playing, but tonight, Sadie just wanted to bask in their evening together.

"Stay," Sadie whispered. "Let's stay here tonight. I don't want to move."

Jagger gathered her in his arms and kissed her temple. "Alright, let's stay."

Sadie nuzzled her face into the crook of his neck and relaxed against him, quickly falling prey to sleep.

Jagger looked down at the beautiful woman beneath him and watched her rest momentarily before slowly pulling out of her and walking across the room to retrieve a blanket from the black armoire by the door. He cleaned up their mess from the evening's festivities and grabbed his cigarettes from his jeans on the floor. He used the red candle's flame that was on the table beside them to light his cigarette and took a seat against the wall on the ground next to Sadie.

As he inhaled slowly, he let the nicotine calm his nerves.

Released the tension in his shoulders.

Smiled.

She was going to marry him.

Jagger reached into his jeans pocket one more time to grab his phone, and within seconds, he was in the **SecretScape** app. They still use it from time to time. Sadie flirts with him through a post, or Jagger uses anonymous ones for ideas for his new novel, which eventually becomes a bestseller.

But tonight, the message he was posting would be nothing short of loving. He glanced over at her and felt his heart tug inside his chest at how fucking lucky he was to have her in his life. He would never, ever allow himself to forget it.

Jagger quickly finished his cigarette, submitted his post, and got under the blanket to hold his soon-to-be-wife close. He breathed in her scent and started to fall asleep to the sound of her heartbeat.

Absolutely ruined, was his last thought as he smiled against her hair.

RebelWearsLeather:

She said yes.

Thank you for reading Serpent Darling.
I hope you enjoyed your time at The Serpent Pit.
If you should feel so inclined, please leave a review on
Amazon or Goodreads.
Follow Pandora Cress on Social Media
TikTok, Threadz & Instagram @authorpandoracress
For up to date info visit my website & join my newsletter
for special events, giveaways, surprise chapters, as well as
Beta and ARC opportunities.

SCAN ME

MASKED
darling

PANDORA CRESS

CHAPTER 1 OF MASKED DARLING

"I'm not going!" Madison called from the other side of her door.

She pressed the length of her body against her bedroom door, barely keeping her best friend from opening it fully. "You can't make me see him!"

Alison stopped pushing against the door and Madison let out a sigh of relief until the door came swinging wide open, causing her to fall backwards onto the plush cream-colored rug next to her bed. Scooting herself backwards, she rested her back against the edge of her bed, smoothing her red hair out of her eyes. Alison strolled right to her and wagged a perfectly manicured finger in her face, "I knew that was why you didn't want to come with me tonight! It's about Kade, isn't it? You have to face him sooner or later, Mads."

Madison pulled her knees up to her chest and softly banged her head against them before looking up at the raven-haired woman towering over her. "You do remember what I did, right? Actually, this party is the least of my problems. I should honestly just switch colleges so I don't have to see him in class either."

Alison dropped to her knees in front of her and rubbed her back. Madison responded to the soothing motion with defeat as tears started to well up, despite her better efforts. "I'm too embarrassed to see him, Al. He probably thinks I'm a sex-crazed pervert."

Alison finally let out a laugh. "Look, I'm not going to judge you for letting your freak flag out, even if it was on school property. But you guys literally run the school paper and you have several classes together. It's best to go to this party and see him now and get whatever awkwardness there is out of the way." The dark-haired beauty tilted Madison's head up and wiped the tears that had just started to spill onto her flushed cheeks with swift strokes of her fingers. "Now, come on. Let's get you cleaned up. Besides, it's a themed party tonight. 'Flasks & Masks' so you can get a few drinks in you without anyone knowing it's you at first."

When Madison stayed seated on the floor, Alison sighed and headed over to her friend's closet, sifting through her options.

"I swear this whole theme is just so Jesse & Christian can get out of providing booze and making everyone bring their own." She looked back at Madison, still sitting on the ground looking distraught. "But it looks like the perfect party for you right now."

Madison gave a slight shrug and raised her hands in surrender. "Fine. But I don't have a flask or a mask."

She looked at the shimmery black mini dress that Alison had her hands on, the one she bought on impulse during their recent shopping trip last weekend. It accentuated all the right curves, featuring a plunging sweetheart neckline that displayed a generous amount of cleavage, and she appreciated how the back fastened with a zipper from both the top to the bottom. It was a far cry from her normal brightly-colored outfits and although she loved it, she was not trying to call attention to herself tonight.

"I can't wear that," Madison said flatly.

"Oh, but you will! This is perfect for tonight," Alison said snatching it off the hanger and laying it on the bed. "I don't think you realize what you do to that boy. It's obvious he likes you. I think you just surprised him, honey." She turned to look at the bottom of the closet for matching shoes. "Now, we need something to put on your feet."

"He caught me touching myself in the office of the Red & Black! I traumatized him," she hissed at her as she finally stood up, even more red curls escaping from the messy bun atop her head. "I was, was…" She trailed off as she put her face in her hands. "I was calling his name, Al," Madison choked out the last words and Alison's mouth hung open at them.

"Oh my god. Madison," Alison gasped while a hand flew to the string of pearls around her neck in slight shock before continuing, "You did not tell me that. You left that important little tidbit out, you little fucker," Alison purred at her, practically swooning over this new information.

"Clearly," Madison remarked. "It's not like I want to relive the single most mortifying experience of my life."

"So, that's why you're so nervous. You can't just chalk this up to some dirty thoughts late at night working on some project while the rest of the school was fast asleep,"

Alison murmured and brushed one of Madison's curls behind her ear. "You were thinking about him and now he knows."

Madison closed her eyes and nodded, totally aware of how screwed she was.

"And he just walked out? He really didn't say anything?" Alison raised an eyebrow at her.

Madison just nodded again.

"Well, after he sees you in this tonight he's bound to say something." Alison smiled and dragged her towards the bedroom down the hall to find her favorite black Louboutins for her to wear with her new black dress.

Kade did not sleep last night at all.

Memories kept flooding back into his mind, over and over again. He knew they had a deadline to meet for the Red and Black's new issue this month and he'd been slacking that week, being dragged around to help his roommates prepare for their big party this weekend. He felt bad that Madison would be stuck with the rest of the work, so on Friday night he decided to go into the office after hours and knock it out before the weekend. He didn't want her there worrying about it on Saturday, hoping she wouldn't have an excuse to miss the party at the apartment. He wanted to see her there, regardless if he was suppressing his feelings for her on the daily.

Kade was turning the corner to the room that connected the office to the dead end of the hallway when he heard his name.

"Kade..." the voice called, although he knew it had to be Madison.

It was late, around midnight and probably not the safest place to be alone if you were a preppy tiny college girl. He started to walk slowly toward the door, taking his time until a sharp, "Oh, god, Kade!" pierced his ears. He practically lunged at the door and flung it wide. He had scarcely placed one foot over the threshold when he shouted, "Madison! Are you -" and came to a complete halt. Kade locked eyes with her for a moment and took a shaky breath as he realized she was alone in the dark classroom.

There was no threat that he could see, except the one to his sanity.

The glow from her laptop was the only thing casting an ethereal glow on her body which was on full display for him. Her white long sleeved blouse hung open slightly, her left hand clutching her right breast through the thin material of her lacy pink bra. He followed the trail of her other arm to where her hand was under her black and brown plaid skirt and his mouth suddenly went dry.

'Jesus Christ, she's touching herself,' Kade thought before he closed his eyes tightly, half from embarrassment and half out of the insane lust that was coursing through his body and straight to his cock. It didn't matter though.

The image of her legs spread wide, one delicate bare foot propped up on the desk and the other barely touching the floor were burned in his mind. Her fingers were still deep inside the prettiest pussy he'd ever seen, the light from the screen making her wet folds look like they were glistening like diamonds.

Afraid to look at her again for fear he might do something stupid, like lift her up and slam her against the desk and take what he'd wanted since they met at his brother's bar on her 21st birthday last year, he turned on his heel and slammed the door shut behind him as he began to walk out of the building in a daze.

So yeah, he hadn't slept at all.

He tried. He really did.

He even jerked off three times throughout the night, thinking he could dull the ache that he felt since realizing that she was masturbating to the idea of him.

Kade let out a deep sigh while visualizing her beautiful flushed face frozen in shock and stared up towards the ceiling of his bedroom.

God, I don't know what I did to deserve that but either it was really good or really fucking bad, he thought as he ran a tired hand down his face in frustration.

Suddenly, a loud knock was at his bedroom door.

"Dude, let's go!" Christian called from the hallway.

"Yeah, K - you've gotta grab the kegs from The Serpent Pit. Oh, and can you ask Camille if she's going to come? She's a babe, man." Jesse chimed in on the other side of his door. Kade rolled his eyes and tossed a black pillow casually over his face as he palmed himself lightly through his boxers, silently cursing himself for being hard again. "She's not into you, Jess. I keep telling you she's all about girls," he muttered into the pillow.

"Doesn't matter, she just hasn't given me a chance yet," Jesse huffed and Kade could hear him retreating down the hall. The sounds of Chris gargling and spitting in the bathroom sink that was across from his room were irritating to say the least, so he reluctantly got himself out of bed.

"Alright, I'm getting up. Text me if there's anything else you can think of that we need while I'm out."

Making his way through the dark blue painted room, thankful that his dick had calmed down, Kade grabbed a pair of jeans off the floor and a black sweater from his closet. It was the end of April in New Jersey, the end of winter hadn't taken all of its chill with it and it still warranted a sweater, if not his trusty leather jacket. The one in which his dad gave him when he decided a life of running around wasn't for him. The one that matched his brother's. The jacket that had defined their lives because being a part of the Renegade Rebels was a lifelong commitment. But Jagger had gotten out of the gang's snare, and now Kade hoped to follow in his footsteps.

"Thanks, man! I'll text you if I think of anything," Chris called out from the bathroom. "I'm excited for tonight. I bet Alison will bring Maddie! You know, that cute blonde you've been pining for the last year?" Kade could hear the grin in Chris's voice. "Maybe you'll finally grow some balls and make a move tonight."

The mention of Madison had all the blood rushing back to the center of his body, his jeans stretching painfully around the obvious indication that he was still under the spell of last night's findings.

Kade gritted his teeth, a frustrated "Goddamn it!" pulled from his throat.

Chris's laughter could be heard drifting down the hallway as Kade closed his eyes and started to count backwards from twenty, a technique his dad used to use when he was trying really hard not to go to jail again.

He glanced down at his erection and sighed.

So much for that.

LAST CALL MENTIONS

First and most importantly, I need to thank you - the readers. Without you, this would just be an idea in my head that was put to paper. But with you, it's become a real place with real people that we care about. At least for a little while, and I can't express how much I love that.

I would not have been able to get this book finished and published without the support of my family. For years they've told me to put down the fanfiction and write a book, so here we are.

To my husband - thank you for always breathing the positive words into me when I'm trying to cut myself down. I wouldn't have made it this far without you.

To my mom - thank you for buying me all the Julie Garwood books you could find in the drugstores and putting up with me riding on your grocery carts pretending to be Belle. We all start somewhere.

And finally, I really have to thank my Beta and ARC readers. You made all the difference. I don't think I would have had the confidence to publish this had it not been for you.

ABOUT THE AUTHOR

Pandora Cress grew up in Atlantic City, NJ surrounded by pageant queens and stretch pants.

Combining her love of horror, the macabre, an unhealthy obsession with quotes, dark romance and sarcasm, you get all the unhinged behavior in her stories. She hopes that her readers can find the passion and the humor in even the darkest of her novels, as the shadows can only be cast by the light.

Pandora currently resides in Pennsylvania with her family where they spend their free time reading, browsing book stores and watching horror movies all year round.

Follow Pandora on TikTok, Threads & Instagram: @authorpandoracress

Made in United States
Orlando, FL
29 October 2024

53229686R00117